SHOT TO HELL

Bounty hunter Jarrett Wade gained his fierce reputation when he defeated the bandit Orlando Pyle in Hamilton. But, several years on, Wade has lost his edge, and is reduced to taking any lowly assignment he can find. A chance to regain his past glory appears when he's offered an apparently simple assignment. He readily accepts — but before he can complete the task, he's gunned down and left for dead . . .

SCOTT CONNOR

SHOT TO HELL

Complete and Unabridged

LINFORD
Leicester

First published in Great Britain in 2014 by
Robert Hale Limited
London

First Linford Edition
published 2017
by arrangement with
Robert Hale
an imprint of
The Crowood Press
Wiltshire

*A catalogue record for this book is available
from the British Library.*

ISBN 978–1–4448–3113–9

Published by
F. A. Thorpe (Publishing)
Anstey, Leicestershire

Set by Words & Graphics Ltd.
Anstey, Leicestershire
Printed and bound in Great Britain by
T. J. International Ltd., Padstow, Cornwall

This book is printed on acid-free paper

1

'Is that you, Jarrett?' the bartender Chester Frey asked.

'Sure is,' Jarrett Wade said. 'Then again, I haven't been in Russell Gulch in years.'

'Many years.' Chester looked Jarrett up and down taking in his paunch, stooped posture and sparse hair. 'Many, many years.'

Jarrett smiled. 'We're all getting older, but I'm hoping you still see and hear as much as you ever did.'

Chester poured Jarrett a whiskey. 'Who are you looking for this time? I hear that the Jackson brothers were in town last week, and Buck Smythe was seen over in Frost Creek last month.'

Jarrett picked up the whiskey and took a long gulp.

'Neither of those.'

'Then you must be after Barney

McCloud. I hear that — '

Jarrett raised a hand, silencing Chester. 'It's none of those men. I'm looking for a young man called Saul Cox.'

Chester shrugged. 'Not heard about him. What did he do?'

'He ran away from home and his pa wants him back.'

Chester laughed and searched Jarrett's eyes as he waited for the punch line to what was clearly a joke, but Jarrett met his gaze until he looked away.

'I don't know nothing about no runaway.'

'Then what about any young men you haven't seen before looking for work?'

Chester frowned. 'You're serious, aren't you? You really are looking for a runaway boy.'

'I have to take any work I can these days.'

Jarrett's comment made Chester look aloft and then nod.

'I heard someone say the very same thing yesterday. This lanky kid offered to paint old Bill Cartwright's stable. I'd never seen him before.'

'That sounds like a good place to start.' Jarrett swirled his whiskey. 'And it'll be good to see Bill again.'

'Bill died four years ago.'

With a wince Jarrett pushed his glass away and headed outside. At the end of the main drag was the stable, which as promised was in need of a lick of paint.

Five surly-looking kids were idling around outside. As he approached, they considered him with lively interest, but before he could question them he saw the young man that interested him.

He was standing at the side of the building, painting the wall in a deep-red colour using long strokes that would probably finish the job within the day.

'You be Saul Cox?' Jarrett said, positioning himself behind him.

The young man flinched, giving a tell-tale sign that no matter what he might claim now, Jarrett had found his quarry.

'You've got the wrong man,' Saul said without turning round. 'And I've got a job to do.'

3

'So have I.'

Saul continued painting using determined strokes while glancing to either side as he clearly judged in which direction he'd flee. Jarrett decided he'd run to the right and head around the back of the stable.

Sure enough, when Saul reached the bottom of his stroke, he dropped the brush and hurried away, but he ran to the left.

Jarrett sighed and set off after him. At the front of the stable Saul scattered the kids, making them turn to watch him flee while hurrying him on his way with catcalls.

When Jarrett reached them he barged the nearest kid aside, which knocked him into two others and upended all three. The other two young men swirled round to glare at him.

'What did you do that for?' one of the kids demanded, blocking Jarrett's path.

'Move aside, kid,' Jarrett grunted.

'Why should I, old-timer?'

Jarrett waved a dismissive hand at

him and moved to follow Saul, who was looking back over his shoulder as he scurried away. Jarrett managed two paces before one of the kids leapt on his back while another one charged him from the side.

Jarrett ignored the onslaught and kept moving forward while one of his assailants tried to tug him backwards and another tried to push him over. But when the rest of the kids joined in the assault he went clattering down on his knees before pitching forward all his length.

With whoops of delight the young men pinned him down. Jarrett struggled to get his breath back until, with a grunt of anger, he slapped both hands down on the ground.

As he forced himself to get back on his feet punches and kicks rained down on him from all sides, until a jarring kick to the chin sent him back down on his chest. The kids must have seen that they'd knocked the fight out of him, as they stopped hitting him.

'See if the old-timer has any money,' one of them said.

Hands rifled through his pockets until a cry of triumph sounded. Jarrett uttered a rueful snarl as he had only a few dollars on him, otherwise he wouldn't be chasing runaways.

Then raised voices sounded as someone noticed his predicament. Footfalls pattered as his assailants scampered away.

Jarrett raised his head to glare at their receding forms. With shame bowing his back he stood up, swaying until he got his balance.

By this time his assailants were slipping away into town, so he dismissed any thoughts of chasing after them and turned to his rescuer, to find that his quarry Saul Cox had returned.

'Are you all right?' Saul asked. 'I never wanted anything like that to happen. I don't who they are, but they've been loitering around all morning making fun of me for working.'

'There's young folk like that in every town, but I'm grateful there's someone like you here,' Jarrett said. He flashed a smile before firming his expression. 'But that's not going to stop me taking you back to your pa.'

Saul set his hands on his hips in irritation, then backed away for a pace so he could look down the main drag. He was the only one who had come to Jarrett's aid and with Jarrett still wincing after his beating, Saul's pensive smile suggested he was thinking about running, but with a sigh he raised his hands.

'I never thought he'd care enough to send someone after me.' He firmed his jaw. 'I guess this proves I can't sort out my problems by running away from them.'

'That's mighty sensible of you.' Jarrett rubbed his sore back and flexed his bruised legs with a groan. 'I didn't want to chase you down and make you suffer any more.'

*   *   *

'What do you want, Marshal?' Quentin Stone said.

The other poker players in the back room of the Horseshoe saloon paid great attention to their cards, but Quentin didn't follow their lead as he leaned back in his chair to glare up at the lawmen.

'Not you, for once,' Marshal Ernest Montague said. 'I'm looking for Denby Grinnell.'

'What's he done this time?'

'Made trouble in my town.'

Quentin sneered. 'We've not seen him. So you can go and do York Stevenson's bidding somewhere else.'

As Ernest glowered at Quentin another one of the players, Doc Cavanaugh, spoke up.

'We've not seen him, Ernest,' he said. 'But he's got no friends over here.'

Ernest moved forward, meaning to question everyone some more after Quentin's impudent jibe, but then the doctor's exact words registered. He glanced at Deputy Hill, who confirmed with a nod that he'd had the same thought: that Cavanaugh had helped them without letting the others know what he'd done.

Hill still moved forward to stand behind Cavanaugh's chair. Then, with a sudden lunge, he tipped the chair backwards so that Cavanaugh looked directly up at him.

'Obliged for your help,' Hill said.

Then he released his hold of the chair letting Cavanaugh topple over on to his back and sending his cards flying away. Cavanaugh floundered on the floor, but Ernest limited himself to shooting Hill a warning glare. Then, without further comment, he joined Hill as he headed outside.

Last night Denby Grinnell, a frequent resident of Hamilton's jailhouse, had been seen sneaking out of a window of the Stevenson Hotel. This morning Lambert Stevenson reported that several customers claimed they'd had money and other valuables stolen from their rooms.

Denby hadn't been at home and, after asking around without success, the lawmen had resorted to the simple process of systematically working their way down one side of Hamilton's main drag. Nobody had seen him and Ernest didn't detect that anyone cared enough about Denby's fate to lie to protect him.

This observation, along with Doc Cavanaugh's comment, suggested Denby was lying low on the other side of the main drag; and Hamilton's troubles usually emanated from one establishment there.

With Hill at his shoulder Ernest headed across the main drag and into the Wild Horse saloon. He walked straight for the stairs at the side of the saloon room and had reached the top before anyone noticed him.

Gerald Gough, the owner, hurried out from behind the bar, but by then Ernest was heading down the corridor. Ernest kicked open the first door. Finding the room empty he moved on to the second, where Hill took over the duties and pushed open the door.

This one was occupied, but not by Denby, so, with cries of consternation and alarm chasing them down the corridor they proceeded to the next room. Two rooms later they found Denby.

He was standing by the window and watching the door with trepidation while holding himself in a position where he could clamber outside quickly.

'You should have climbed out the window while you still could,' Ernest said. 'Just like you did in the Stevenson hotel yesterday.'

'I never stole nothing in that place yesterday,' Denby said.

'Except you know something was stolen, you know it was stolen from the Stevenson hotel, and you were seen slipping out of the window.' Ernest advanced a long pace. 'Then you went into hiding.'

'Of course I did. The last time something went missing you blamed me.' Denby set his hands on his hips with increased confidence as Gerald arrived in the doorway. 'And I never did nothing that time either.'

With Denby looking at Gerald for support, Gerald stepped into the room.

'You heard Denby,' Gerald said. 'He had nothing to do with this robbery, if there even was one. I wouldn't have given him a room otherwise.'

Ernest snorted. 'Except, whether he's guilty or not, you helped Denby go into hiding and that isn't the most sensible thing you've ever done. Standing in the way of the law will be even worse.'

'I've never stood in the way of the law. I don't need to.' Gerald sneered. 'I pay you enough not to stand in *my* way.'

'We're old friends, Gerald, and we do have an understanding, but when your behaviour affects decent folk like Lambert Stevenson, that understanding ends.'

'I never knew you cared about Lambert. I thought you only did what his brother York told you to do.'

With Gerald being the second man to make that insult tonight, Ernest couldn't keep his anger in check. He advanced on Gerald with a snarl.

Gerald stood his ground as he weighed up the situation, but the determined look in Ernest's eye made him give Denby a resigned look. Without any more complaints he backed away into the corridor.

'It looks as if you'll have to throw me in a cell,' Denby said, as Hill closed the door and stood guard. 'But that won't help you get back whatever was stolen, because I haven't got it. I don't even know what was stolen.'

Ernest didn't know this either, as Lambert Stevenson had been vague about the items that had been taken, presumably because the victims had been vague too, as they sought to profit from the unfortunate incident.

'For once I agree with you. Last time, throwing you in a cell didn't help nothing.' Ernest walked across the room and then contemplated his right hand as he bunched it. 'Perhaps this time I should try a different method.'

Denby considered Ernest, then Hill. Both men glared at him until he gave a resigned sigh, lowering his head and making Ernest glance at Hill in triumph.

Unfortunately Denby's apparent capitulation had been only a bluff. He twisted round, slapped a hand on the window-sill and moved to clamber out of the window.

Hill scrambled for his gun and a moment later a gunshot tore out, echoing in the small room, making Denby straighten while raising a hand to clutch his back.

Denby groaned pitifully and met Ernest's gaze with a pained look that registered an emotion, perhaps disappointment. Then he toppled forward through the window. A few moments later a thud sounded.

Ernest turned to Hill, who slipped his gun back in its holster.

'He looked like he was going for a concealed weapon,' Hill said.

'I didn't see that.' Ernest rocked his head from side to side. 'But he was clearly trying to escape.'

Hill shrugged. 'You're the boss. Take your pick.'

Ernest frowned. Then he moved on to the window and looked down.

Denby was lying on his back. He wasn't moving while people gravitated towards him and others looked up at the window with concern.

'Perhaps we'll go for him doing both,' Ernest said.

Hill joined him at the window and looked down. He chuckled.

'Either way, it doesn't look as if we'll get any answers out of him now.'

Behind them the door flew open and Gerald came storming in. He had numerous customers in tow and their presence bolstered his confidence as he stood with his feet placed wide apart in a defiant stance.

'Denby was no threat to nobody,' Gerald said. 'You didn't have to shoot him.'

Ernest shrugged and smiled at everyone.

'I prefer to think that this was another successful conclusion to an investigation,' he said.

2

'Independence seems a mighty fine town,' Jarrett said when they approached Saul Cox's farm. 'I can't see why you'd want to run away to a two-bit place like Russell Gulch.'

'I wasn't running away from a place,' Saul said. 'It was a person.'

On the journey back to Independence Jarrett hadn't asked for an explanation of why he'd had to track Saul down, treating him as he would a fugitive from justice. But over the last few hours his young companion had become increasingly agitated, so Jarrett had shown an interest in his predicament to find out whether he might cause him a problem before he reached Independence.

'Your pa looked concerned about you, otherwise he wouldn't have paid me fifty dollars to find you.'

'Fifty dollars! That old varmint Brett hasn't got fifty dollars.'

'You shouldn't talk about your father that way.'

'Brett's not my father.' Saul gazed at Jarrett until he nodded, then he continued: 'My mother married him when I was young, but she died last year and since then his temper and drinking have got out of hand. I had to get away.'

'What happened to your real father?'

'I don't know. I don't even know who he was.' Saul shrugged. 'Or at least I didn't until last month, and that's what tipped him over the edge.'

'Go on.'

'I found some letters in my mother's belongings. They were from this man and the things he wrote . . . ' Saul sighed. 'They made me think he could be my father, so I decided to go and find him. I figured getting some work and some money first would help, but I never got to finish what I started.'

Saul shot Jarrett an aggrieved glare. Jarrett rode on for a while so he could choose his next words carefully.

'How old are you?'

'Seventeen, come the fall.'

'Then you're old enough to make your way in the world, but it'll be hard. While you're working on your pa's farm you're learning valuable skills and you're getting stronger. So take every opportunity to learn and to save any money you can get your hands on. Then choose your time to leave and you'll get away no matter who Brett sends after you. And you'll be able to earn a living when you get there.'

Saul relaxed and offered him a grateful smile.

'That's good advice.'

'So do you have a place to start looking?'

'Yeah. The letters were from a man called Ernest Montague.'

Jarrett raised an eyebrow in surprise. 'Marshal Ernest Montague from Hamilton?'

Saul smiled. 'I'd asked around and someone told me he was a lawman, although he wasn't when he wrote to my mother.'

Jarrett turned in the saddle to face Saul.

'I knew Ernest some years back and I can't say that you look like him.' Jarrett shrugged when Saul frowned. 'On the other hand, when I knew him Ernest was the kind of man who'd go back and help someone, even if that man was chasing him.'

Saul licked his lips, but he couldn't avoid a massive grin breaking out.

'How did you know him?'

'I'm a bounty hunter . . . ' Jarrett sighed. 'I *used* to be a bounty hunter. Ernest was protecting Tyrone Hendrick's stockyard when I brought in the Orlando Pyle gang.'

'I've never heard of them.'

'You would have been a lot younger when I shot them to hell.'

'And you've not seen Ernest since?'

Jarrett rode on for a while, wondering whether to explain about the event that had caused his own demise. As in a few more minutes he'd be parting company with Saul, he shook his head.

'Nope. Not been back to Hamilton in five years.'

Saul looked at Jarrett oddly, suggesting he'd heard the concern in his tone, but he said nothing and they continued in silence to the farm. As they rode through the gates Saul's shoulders became bowed and he slowed down, so Jarrett directed an encouraging wink at him and in return Saul smiled wanly.

Brett was already standing outside with a hand to his brow, having clearly seen them approaching from some distance. His expression was as dour as it had been when he'd given Jarrett his mission.

'You found him quickly,' Brett said when they'd drawn up.

'Saul was in the first place I looked,' Jarrett said. 'He fetched up in Russell Gulch, and you'll be pleased to hear he was working hard.'

'I'm surprised he knows how to.'

Saul lowered his head even further

20

and clambered down from his horse. Then he slouched towards Brett, who glowered at him.

When Saul reached Brett he met his eye for a moment, then hurried on towards the house. Brett turned to watch him go by until, almost as an after-thought, he clipped the back of his head with the flat of his hand.

Saul stumbled and went to his knees. Brett, having unleashed his anger, muttered an oath and stood over him with his fists raised.

'That's enough,' Jarrett said. 'Saul's sorry for what he did and you hitting him won't make him any sorrier.'

'Be quiet,' Brett muttered. 'You're not his father.'

'I'm not.'

The deliberate manner in which Jarrett had intoned his response made Brett sneer at him, as if he'd understood some of its implications. Brett's attention no longer being on him, Saul took advantage of the distraction and scurried into the house.

Brett ignored him and withdrew a handful of bills from his pocket.

'You've got no reason to be on my land now. Take your money and go.'

Jarrett resisted the urge to offer Brett some advice on how he should treat Saul, as he reckoned anything he said would only make life worse for the young man. He moved his horse on and reached down for the money.

He counted it, then glared at Brett.

'We agreed on fifty dollars. You've only given me twenty.'

'It seems to me you didn't have to look for long. Saul was only in Russell Gulch.'

'We agreed on fifty dollars and that's all I'd have asked for whether he was in the first place I looked or the hundredth.'

'Except he was in the first, which means I could have got anyone to find him. That's only worth twenty dollars. Take it and be thankful.'

Jarrett pocketed the money. 'Obliged for the part payment. I'll leave when I have the rest.'

'Then you'll have a long wait.' Brett chuckled. 'You see, I haven't got fifty dollars.'

Jarrett weighed up the merits of arguing, but Brett's smirk suggested his last comment had been truthful. He shook his head.

'How you could be the father of that hardworking, decent young man, I'll never know.'

He waited until Brett's eyes flared in anger, then he turned his horse away. At the gate he looked over his shoulder, but Brett had now disappeared from view.

Jarrett wished Saul well and hoped he'd take his advice about leaving at a time of his choosing and after planning his escape properly. Then he moved on to town.

★　★　★

Three hours later he was standing at the bar in the Hard Knocks saloon with a whiskey glass in his hand.

The liquor was still failing to raise his spirits when a small and wiry man wearing pebble-glasses bustled into the saloon. He glanced Jarrett's way, but he still spoke with a couple of men until one of them pointed at Jarrett.

'Would I be right in thinking you used to be Jarrett Wade?' the man asked as he joined him at the bar.

'Still am the last time I looked,' Jarrett said, leaning over his glass.

The man uttered a nervous cough. 'Perhaps I didn't phrase my question well. I meant, did you once use to be the bounty hunter Jarrett Wade?'

'Yup.'

'That would explain why you tracked down Saul Cox so efficiently and, so I have gathered, you brought him back in good time and in good health.'

Jarrett took a sip of his whiskey. 'You gather plenty.'

'Of that you are most correct.' The man held out his hand, but Jarrett ignored it. The man coughed again. 'I should introduce myself properly. I'm

Ascott Beadley and I'm a lawyer with the renowned firm of — '

'If you've got work for me, I'd be obliged if you'd explain yourself quicker. If you haven't, I'd be obliged if you'd go away and let me enjoy my drink in peace.'

'I do have work for you, but I would prefer it if we could talk in private.' Ascott offered a fragile smile. 'You can finish your drink first, if you like.'

'Obliged.' Jarrett knocked back his whiskey.

Ten minutes later he was sitting in Ascott's office.

With a jaundiced eye, Jarrett watched the officious little man go about his business, which involved rooting around in his safe and then moving paper around his desk without achieving any discernible change in the order there.

When he had arranged everything to his liking, Ascott looked at him over the top of his pebble-glasses.

'I wish you to deliver an important document to Lambert Stevenson.'

Ascott picked up an old parchment from his desk. It was covered in text and it had a seal at the bottom.

Jarrett looked aloft and then shrugged.

'I met him once, but I can't remember when. My memory isn't what it used to be. I presume you know where Lambert is.'

'I do,' Ascott said, giving an irritated grunt as if to suggest he'd had his speech worked out in the same meticulous manner as he'd laid out his documents and Jarrett had distracted him. 'The content and intent of the document are not important for you to know. All you do need to know is that you must deliver it into Lambert's hands and nobody else's.'

'I need to know one other thing.' Jarrett smiled. 'How much do I get paid?'

'Lambert will pay you fifty dollars on receipt of the document.' Ascott returned the smile. 'But I'm aware of your recent experience with Brett Cox and I hope you'll be pleased to hear that in addition I'll pay you fifty dollars on acceptance of this duty.'

Jarrett nodded, so Ascott busied himself with folding the parchment and placing it in a slim metal case. Then, using a candle, he dripped sealing-wax over the clasp, then blew on the seal until it had set.

When he was satisfied that the case had been sealed securely, he held it out. Jarrett found that the case was small enough to slip into an inside pocket of his jacket.

The payment went in another inside pocket, and Jarrett awaited any further instructions. But by the time Ascott had made him sign for the document and for the money in several places he was eager to move on.

'Where is Lambert Stevenson?' he asked, getting to his feet.

'He currently resides in Hamilton.'

Jarrett had been nodding while moving to the door so he could avoid Ascott waylaying him with any more irrelevant duties, but the answer made him pause.

'I haven't been there for many years,' he said, his tone as low as it had been earlier when he'd spoken briefly to Saul about his previous visit to this town.

Ascott narrowed his eyes, clearly noting Jarrett's concern.

'I hope you have no problem with returning there.'

'I guess I don't.' Jarrett patted the bulge in his pocket. 'After all, I've signed for the money.'

3

Jarrett was two miles out of Independence when he drew his horse to a halt.

His route would take him past Brett Cox's farm and for several minutes he gazed thoughtfully at the house. Then, with a sigh, he veered towards it.

Like yesterday, Brett was outside and saw him coming. Unlike yesterday he scurried inside and by the time Jarrett reached the gate he had emerged with a rifle in hand.

'I told you yesterday,' Brett shouted, 'I don't have fifty dollars. I paid you everything I had.'

Jarrett rode in and dismounted outside the house.

'Then you'll be pleased to hear I don't want the rest of my money.'

'So what do you want?'

Jarrett rubbed his jaw, as if considering, then offered Brett a placating smile, which made him lower the rifle a mite.

'The way I see it, you agreed to pay me money for a service. Now you've gone back on our deal. So I reckon I should go back on our deal, too.'

Brett furrowed his brow. 'How can you do that?'

'That's simple.' Jarrett faced the house and raised his voice. 'Saul, get out here now. It's time to leave.'

'Leave?' Brett spluttered. 'You're not taking my son away.'

'It seems only fair. You wouldn't pay me when I'd found him, so I'll help him disappear again.'

Brett stared at him in shock, his grinding jaw suggesting he was weighing up whether to call Jarrett's bluff or not, but Jarrett didn't care what he decided as he wasn't bluffing. Brett still hadn't found a suitable retort when Saul emerged from the house.

He had a bulging bag over one shoulder, with clothes poking out of the top, but he kept his head lowered as he gave Brett a wide berth. Any residual doubts Jarrett had about coming here fled when Saul looked up, revealing a livid bruise on his cheek and a split lip that was still bloody.

'You're going nowhere, boy,' Brett said.

'You're the one who's going nowhere,' Saul said. 'I've got plenty of places to go.'

Brett snarled in anger and turned away from confronting Jarrett. He swung the rifle round and raised the stock. Then he advanced on Saul, but when he moved to hit Saul Jarrett hurried over and grabbed the rifle stopping it a foot from Saul's head.

The two men strained for supremacy, neither man getting the upper hand until Saul moved in and kicked Brett's shin. As Brett was concentrating on rebuffing Jarrett the blow took him by surprise, and he stumbled.

Jarrett helped Brett on his way with a shove to the shoulder, making his opponent fall on his back where he lay glaring up at them. The rifle had stayed in

Jarrett's hand: now he hurled it aside.

The moment the weapon hit the dust Brett kicked off from the ground. Head down, he charged Jarrett, forcing him to step back quickly.

He couldn't avoid Brett's manic charge and Brett's shoulders slammed into his hips, toppling him backwards. Both men went down with Brett on top, pressing down on Jarrett.

Brett's breath was sour and his eyes were wild and glaring, but the fall had knocked the wind out of Jarrett's chest and he struggled to free himself.

Red-faced, Brett put both hands to Jarrett's throat and pressed down. Jarrett grabbed Brett's wrists and tugged.

At first Brett did not yield to his firm grip, but then, as Jarrett's lungs began demanding air Brett flinched and slackened his hands. Seizing his chance, Jarrett put all his strength into a wild bucking of his hips, knocking Brett aside.

Then he squirmed his way clear of Brett's body and, on hands and knees, he scrambled away. When he gained his feet, he saw that it was not he who had made Brett relent.

Saul had gathered up the discarded rifle, and he had aimed it at Brett's chest.

'You won't shoot your father,' Brett snarled.

'I wouldn't,' Saul said. 'But you're not my father.'

Brett advanced on Saul, forcing Jarrett to draw his six-shooter.

'That's far enough,' he said.

Brett glanced over his shoulder and sneered when he saw that he now had two guns aimed at him, but he did stop.

'So the two of you have joined forces to rob me, have you?'

'I'm not robbing you, but I am keeping the twenty dollars for my trouble.'

Brett shrugged, as if he'd not been referring to the payment, but as he made no further attempt to confront them, Jarrett caught Saul's eye. Saul nodded and hurried away to the barn.

When Saul returned he had collected his horse and had disposed of the rifle.

Without even looking again at Brett, he mounted up and moved on.

Jarrett reckoned he had the right idea in extricating themselves from this situation quickly, but he kept his gun on Brett until Saul was through the gate.

'This isn't over,' Brett said as Jarrett walked to his horse sideways, so as to keep him in sight.

'It is,' Jarrett said. 'It was always going to end this way. When you hired me, you just delayed the inevitable by a few months. Take my advice and — '

'I've had enough of your advice. Your advice made Saul leave.'

Jarrett didn't reckon he could achieve anything by trying to talk sense into Brett, so he said nothing as he mounted up. Then, before he moved on, he limited himself to flashing a glare at Brett, warning him not to follow them.

By the time he'd reached the gate Saul was slowing down to let him catch up with him, but behind them Brett was emerging from the barn, and he'd already found his rifle.

'Find anything interesting?' Deputy Hill asked when Marshal Ernest Montague returned to the law office after searching Denby Grinnell's house.

Ernest threw the box of interesting finds on to his desk with a clatter.

'I found some money and a few trinkets,' he said.

Hill glanced at Denby's body, which was lying beneath a blanket in the corner of the office.

'So Denby was guilty, after all.'

'It's looking more likely.' Ernest held out a hand. 'And I'll know that for sure when I've read his signed confession.'

'What signed confession?'

'The confession you extracted from our prisoner while I was collecting evidence.'

Hill laughed, but when Ernest's expression grew stern, he shrugged and headed over to Denby's body. He removed the blanket and dragged the body to his desk beside which, after some manoeuvring, he deposited it on a chair.

The body started to slip to the floor, so Hill looped an arm over the back of the chair and wedged the legs between the chair and the side of the desk. Then he stood back to consider the effect.

Aside from the head lolling to the side so that one ear rested on a shoulder, Denby's body did look like a prisoner who'd been brought in for questioning. So he walked round to the other side of the desk and collected some papers.

'So, Denby,' he asked, peering over his desk, 'do you want to confess to all of your heinous crimes?'

Hill waited for a few moments, then glanced at Ernest, who gave an encouraging nod. So he began writing. With that matter in hand, Ernest searched through the items he'd acquired.

There was little of value, but, thankfully, by the time he'd finished looking news of his return must have spread as the hotel owner Lambert Stevenson arrived with Doc Cavanaugh in tow.

'The doctor tells me you're now sure

Denby robbed my hotel,' Lambert said.

'I sure am,' Ernest said.

'But I'm not pleased that this trivial matter ended so violently. Denby only . . . ' Lambert trailed off when he noticed Denby's body for the first time. He shot a horrified glance at Cavanaugh, who nodded. 'But he's dead!'

'I agree that Denby's enjoyed better days.'

Cavanaugh walked across the office to look more closely at the body. A gasp of disgust escaped his lips.

'Denby may have been a thief,' Cavanaugh said, 'but he deserves more dignity than being propped up in a chair like that.'

'He'll get to lie down later, but only after Hill's finished questioning him. If he's not cooperative we may have to rough him up.'

Hill looked up and waved his half-written statement at Cavanaugh.

'And with any luck,' he said, 'he might confess to a few more unexplained crimes, too.'

Cavanaugh shook his head sadly. Lambert stared at the deputy in horror, then he turned to Ernest.

'This is . . . is . . . ' Lambert waved his arms as he struggled to find the right words to express his anger, so Ernest smiled.

'An outrage? An insult? Or is it my duty to apprehend and deal with men like Denby?'

'Your duty doesn't call for this.' Lambert sighed and stood back to face Ernest. 'These days you seem to take delight in treating everyone with contempt.'

'I treat outlaws with contempt. I treat the victims of their crimes with dignity.' Ernest gestured at the box. 'So look in here and you might find a few items that went missing.'

'Only money was stolen, and I'm not even sure about that. The patrons in the rooms that got broken into were vague about what they'd lost.'

'We both know what they hoped to gain out of the situation, but take whatever you reckon will keep them quiet.' Ernest winked. 'That deathly pallor Denby's got right now makes me think he's got no further use for any of it.'

Lambert winced and the two men looked at each other until, with a grunt, Lambert picked up the bills and coins. As he counted through them, Ernest licked his lips, pleased to have won this small victory in getting Lambert to accept the money.

When he'd finished Lambert took thirty dollars, leaving about twenty dollars along with the trinkets.

'This should smooth over any problems,' he said. Without meeting Ernest's eye he turned to the door.

'I'm pleased to have been of service,' Ernest called after him.

Lambert stopped for a moment, then he walked to the door. Ernest, smiling, watched him go, then he turned to Cavanaugh, who took his time before speaking.

'What's happened to you, Ernest?' he said with a low tone. 'Lambert was right. When we all worked at the stock-yard, you used to treat people fairly.'

'You know what happened to me,' Ernest said, matching the doctor's low tone. 'Back in those days I did treat everyone well, but then Orlando Pyle came along and I lost their respect.'

'We all lost plenty during those raids, but York Stevenson kept faith in you. He reckoned you were the right man for this job, and back then I agreed with him.'

'And now?'

Cavanaugh sighed. 'We're old friends, Ernest, and I reckon we've known each other for long enough for me to tell you the truth. You've associated with the wrong people for so long you no longer know what's right any more. Stop shooting up little men like Denby Grinnell while treading carefully around men like Gerald Gough.'

'Obliged for the advice. Anything more?'

Cavanaugh glanced at Hill, who had just finished writing the confession.

'Remember who your friends are.'

Cavanaugh gave Ernest a long look and then headed to the door. Ernest watched him leave, dismissing the matter with a sigh. He turned to his deputy.

'Want to check this?' Hill asked, waving the confession.

'Nope,' Ernest said.

'So is there anything else I can do tonight?'

'Sure. See what you can sell these items for.' Ernest placed in his desk drawer the twenty dollars Lambert had left, then pushed the box of trinkets towards Hill. 'It looks like we made a profit.'

* * *

'How long will it take us to reach Hamilton?' Saul asked when he and Jarrett had made camp for the night.

'Four days, taking the most direct route,' Jarrett said. 'That'll be the safest option.'

They hadn't seen Brett again since leaving the farm, but Saul had frequently looked over his shoulder, thinking it was probable that he'd follow them.

'And you'll stay with me all the way?'

Jarrett hadn't told Saul about the document he had to deliver and his old cautious nature meant he saw no reason to mention it now.

'I have business that way, so we're together until Hamilton. Then you're on your own, whether Marshal Ernest Montague takes kindly to your news or not.'

Saul frowned and withdrew a sheaf of letters from his pocket.

'I'm obliged for your help, but whether he likes what I've got to tell him or not, I'm not sure what I want to do.'

'I wouldn't expect you to know when it's so uncertain how Ernest will react to what's in those letters. Once you know that, you'll be clearer in your mind.' Jarrett watched Saul smile, seemingly approving of this attitude. 'If you want, I'll introduce you to him before I move on.'

Saul looked down at the letters and

then at Jarrett. With a frown, as if dismissing the thought of asking him to read the letters and offer an opinion, he slipped them back in his pocket.

'I'd prefer to approach him in my own time.'

'Do that, but don't leave it too long. Unwelcome tasks have a habit of becoming bigger in the mind than they are.'

Saul looked him in the eye. 'Are you talking about my problem, or about you going back to Hamilton? Because I thought you looked concerned about that yesterday.'

Jarrett laughed. 'You're a perceptive young man. And, yes, I have misgivings about heading that way again, but now is the right time to put those misgivings aside.'

They sat silently for a while. When Jarrett seemed not to be offering anything more, Saul leaned forward.

'What happened there?' he prompted. 'All I know is what you said yesterday that you brought in the Orlando Pyle gang.'

'You've got a good memory, too.' Jarrett sighed and he gazed at the stars as he pondered about whether he wanted to explain. 'That was my most successful bounty hunt, but in other ways it was my worst. Maybe without it I wouldn't be reduced to accepting jobs that pay fifty dollars, if I'm lucky, and helping runaways get away from home.'

'Then perhaps something good came out of your bad fortune.'

Jarrett smiled, liking the sound of that way of thinking. Feeling in a magnanimous mood, he waited only a few moments before explaining himself.

'Five years ago everything in Hamilton revolved around Tyrone Hendrick's stockyard. The Orlando Pyle gang preyed on its operations for months. Nobody could get close to them, never mind stop them. Tyrone kept raising the bounty and I was tempted. I was heading for Hamilton when I had some luck. I happened across Orlando preparing another raid.'

Saul's eyes lit up as he listened to this

tale and he leaned forward, eager to hear more.

'I assume that was his bad luck?'

'Sure was. I took two of the gang before they even knew they were being ambushed. Two others panicked in the dark and I dispatched them. That left Orlando Pyle. We traded gunfire for a while until he bolted for freedom. I gunned him down.'

'That sounds like a success.'

'It was. I got drunk for a month and I never paid for a single drink. Then I collected the bounty and got drunk for another month. I reckoned I'd never have to go on another manhunt again, and, in a way, I didn't. Five thousand dollars could have been enough to last a lifetime, but I spent some here and I gambled the rest there, until one day it'd all gone.'

Jarrett looked aloft and laughed as he recalled some of the many good times he'd had, making Saul smile.

'So what was the problem?'

'When I needed money again I

decided to go after another bounty. I thought I could use my old skills, but while I'd been busy enjoying myself, I'd lost my edge. I barely escaped with my life from that first encounter with an outlaw, and I've been going downhill ever since.'

'It sounds as if Hamilton might be the right place to go to get back your confidence.'

Jarrett frowned. 'I don't reckon so. I have a reputation there. Everyone remembers me as the man who brought in the Orlando Pyle gang, the finest bounty hunter in the state, a hero. Except I'm not that man any more, so why would I want reminding of that?'

'Perhaps because from what I've seen you still are that man.'

Jarrett opened his mouth to pour scorn on this comment, but then thought better of it.

'Go to sleep, kid. We'll be travelling fast and we've got an early start tomorrow.'

4

Hamilton had changed.

Five years ago, when Jarrett had tired of the adulation and had left, the town had been just a handful of buildings huddled beside Tyrone Hendrick's stockyard.

York Stevenson now ran that yard and the town had been boosted by two other stockyards. Numerous buildings sprawled out to the south of the railroad, which caused Jarrett to get lost on the way to the Stevenson hotel, where the lawyer had booked him a room.

Nobody looked their way, relieving his worry that he would be recognized and so attract unwelcome attention. After backtracking twice through the maze of streets, Jarrett drew up outside the hotel.

'I hope I won't be here long,' Jarrett said. He dismounted and reached into his pocket. 'Once I've finished my business I'll move on. So if I don't see you again, accept this. It's only ten dollars, half of the amount Brett paid me, but it should help.'

'I'll find work,' Saul said. 'I'll be fine.'

Jarrett thrust out the money. 'Take it. This will let you stay here for a while and give you time to sort out your business.'

Saul sighed and took the offered bills.

'I'm obliged, but I reckon I'll sort this out straight away. You waited five years to return here and it doesn't look as if your worst fears will be realized. Maybe it'll be the same for me.'

Jarrett nodded, pleased despite his concern about being in Hamilton again that the young man appeared to have gained something from riding with him for a few days.

'Then let's take a room and get our lives sorted out.'

Saul considered the money and then the imposing Stevenson hotel. He shook his head.

'I need to make this money last. I'll find a cheaper place to stay.' He held out a hand. 'Thank you for helping me.'

Jarrett took the hand, wished Saul well and made his way to the entrance. At the door he glanced over his shoulder and noted that Saul was looking down the main drag at the law office. Then he headed inside.

After he'd been hollering for attention for some moments, a man slouched in from a back room. He had a bored air.

'What do you want?' he said around a yawn, after introducing himself as Quentin Stone.

'I'm Jarrett Wade.'

Quentin straightened up. Then, all bustling activity, he got Jarrett to sign in and informed him that a message that he'd be coming had been sent ahead.

'I've reserved the finest room in the building and it's yours for as many nights as you need it.'

'If Lambert's available I may not need it for even the one night.'

'Ah, Lambert didn't know when you'd arrive, so he's not here now and he won't be back until this evening.'

'Then I'll probably need the room for the one night. Be sure to tell Lambert where I am.'

Quentin grunted and returned to his business, but as Jarrett walked away Quentin continued looking at him from the corner of his eye. When Jarrett reached the stairs Quentin scurried to the front door.

Jarrett climbed the stairs three at a time and hurried on to his room. By the time he looked out of the window, Quentin had reached the other side of the main drag.

Quentin spoke with a group of three men, who nodded and looked at Jarrett's hotel room window. They were too far away for him to see them clearly, but Jarrett was thankful he'd stayed in the shadows. Then Quentin hurried back across the road.

The men talked amongst themselves, then, their debate seemingly concluded, one man walked away. The others leaned back against the wall and, in a casual manner, they resumed their apparent idling behaviour.

A minute passed before one man glanced up at Jarrett's window; then the other man looked his way, too.

Jarrett moved away from the window.

'It seems I was right to be worried,' he said to himself.

* * *

The young man had been loitering outside on the boardwalk for over an hour before he opened the law office door, but then he had to step aside as Quentin Stone came bustling past him.

'You should have come in earlier,' Ernest said, looking past Quentin at the young man. 'Now you'll have to wait your turn. Quentin here works for Lambert Stevenson and that means he's an important man. So everybody has to step aside when he's going somewhere.'

The young man flashed him a thankful smile, but Quentin snarled.

'You'll do well not to rile me,' he snapped. 'There's been another robbery in the Stevenson hotel.'

'It seems to me that for the sake of his patrons Lambert should be more careful.'

'He doesn't need any lectures from you, but the more important point is that if there's been another robbery, that means Denby Grinnell didn't carry out the last one.'

'That's a mighty big assumption. Luckily for the townsfolk of Hamilton I don't jump to premature conclusions. I investigate all crimes properly and my deputy gathered a signed confession for the last robbery. I'll deal with the latest robbery using the same diligence.'

Deputy Hill chuckled, making Quentin flash an irritated glare at him before he walked to the door. In his haste to leave he again barged the young man aside.

Ernest gestured at Hill to join him in

following Quentin, but the young man belatedly plucked up the courage to approach him.

'Are you Marshal Ernest Montague?' he asked in an uncertain tone.

'I sure am, son,' Ernest said, eyeing the departing Quentin through the window. 'But you'll have to explain your problem quickly. As you can see, Quentin has a problem and that means I now have a problem.'

Despite his warning the young man fidgeted from foot to foot nervously while glancing around the law office. As he looked uncomfortable about stating his business, Deputy Hill pointed at the door.

'I'll wait outside,' he said.

'I'll be with you in a moment,' Ernest said. He raised an eyebrow while taking slow steps towards the door, but the young man still waited until Hill had left before he replied.

'My name's Saul Cox,' he said, his hopeful gaze suggesting he thought this would explain his reason for being here.

'I'm afraid I've never heard of you before.'

Saul lowered his gaze and his shoulders slumped. As no explanation seemed to be forthcoming Ernest put a hand to the door. This appeared to impress upon Saul the urgency of the situation and he cleared his throat.

'My mother was Malvina Cox, although you would have known her when she was Malvina Kipling.'

The name made Ernest stomp to a halt.

'I haven't seen Malvina for nigh on sixteen years, perhaps more. How is . . . ?'

Ernest trailed off when he registered Saul's exact words and accordingly, Saul provided a sympathetic frown.

'She died last winter. I've been sorting through her belongings and I came across some letters you sent her.' Saul flashed a brief smile.

Ernest's stomach lurched and he was glad he was holding on to the door as that stopped him from stumbling.

'How old are you, S-Saul?'

'I'm seventeen come the fall, sir.'

They considered each other until from the corner of his eye Ernest saw Hill outside craning his neck to see what was delaying him.

'I'm afraid I do have to go, but we'll talk, later.'

Ernest ushered Saul out of the office and, now that he had stated his reason for coming to the law office, Saul gave a relieved sigh. Then he left at a brisk trot and without meeting Ernest's eye again.

Ernest watched him hurry away down the boardwalk until, with a shake of his head, he forced himself to concentrate on the matter at hand. Hill looked at him oddly, but Ernest didn't explain as they hurried after Quentin and in the opposite direction to Saul.

At the hotel Quentin led them up to what he promised was Lambert's finest room. It looked like one of the four rooms that had been robbed before but, unlike after that incident when there had been no sign that anything untoward had happened, this time the room had been ransacked.

Furniture had been toppled, cupboard doors hung askew, and the bedclothes had been dragged on to the floor.

'Anything missing?' Hill asked.

'With this mess it's hard to tell,' Quentin said.

'Whose room is it?'

'I can't remember the name. He only booked in an hour ago.'

Hill looked at Quentin with an eyebrow raised, and Quentin looked away, suggesting he had just lied. He scurried off to find the law officers a name.

'What do you reckon?' Ernest asked when the door had closed.

'This looks different from the last time,' Hill said. 'So there's no reason to suppose we got it wrong when we blamed Denby.'

'Denby acted like he was guilty. Then again, he could have been guilty of plenty of things.' Ernest pondered the situation. 'Was this one of the rooms that got broken into the last time?'

Hill turned to the door, then gestured, seemingly recalling the rooms and their positions in the hotel.

'I don't think so, but then again I don't think this one was occupied then. Denby started at the east side of the hotel and worked his way towards this room.'

'Or he started here, and after finding it wasn't occupied he worked his way west.'

Hill thought some more. 'I wonder if he was looking for a particular room, but in the dark he wasn't sure where it was and he finished up here?'

Ernest smiled. 'And as he didn't find what he was looking for, someone came back later to finish the job?'

'This mess suggests the second thief might have found what he wanted.'

'I like your thinking, except for the fact that the person in this room only booked in an hour ago.'

Hill frowned and he continued looking around the room as he reconsidered his theory. Ernest reckoned that Hill had been close to the truth: that the two incidents were connected, even if he couldn't see how yet, but by the time Quentin returned Hill had brightened.

'Did this room get booked in advance?' he asked Quentin.

'It was, although I wasn't sure when it'd be occupied,' Quentin said, his nervous tone making it clear he'd worked out the significance of this fact before Hill looked at Ernest in triumph.

Ernest didn't need to state in front of Quentin how this completed the details of their developing theory.

Denby knew a room had been booked, but he wasn't a resourceful thief, so he didn't know which one or when its owner would arrive. Denby had a specific item he wanted to steal, so he'd disturbed the other rooms to create confusion.

Now someone who had more determination than Denby had returned to steal the targeted item and they'd been more thorough. Although it was unclear whether the thief had found what he was looking for, one other question remained.

'Whose room is it?' he asked.

'Jarrett Wade's,' Quentin said.

This familiar name from many years ago made Ernest pause for the second time today, giving him cause to ponder whether Saul's appearance with news of someone from his past might be connected. His making no reply caused Hill to look at him oddly, until Ernest shook the thought away.

'I reckon we've learnt everything we can here,' Hill said. 'We now need to go after whoever did this.'

'We do,' Ernest said. 'But now Jarrett Wade's back in town I reckon someone will pay for this before sunup.'

5

Someone was approaching.

With only the low moonlight illuminating the terrain, the rider was no more than fifty yards away before Jarrett recognized him as Lambert Stevenson.

As he couldn't trust Quentin Stone Jarrett had sneaked into Lambert's office earlier. He'd left him a note to meet him after sundown a quarter-mile out of town at an abandoned shack he'd seen on the way in.

Then he'd crept out of town, afoot, and before it'd got dark he'd roamed the area planning his escape route if the exchange were to go wrong. This location was ideal.

On one side a steep slope led down to the rail-tracks, too steep for anyone to climb. Open ground on the other three sides ensured that he'd notice anyone approaching.

As it had turned out, since he had come here it had been quiet and he hadn't seen the men who had been watching his hotel room. It was now three hours after sundown and Lambert was riding openly, though peering ahead as if he were the one who was concerned about trouble.

Jarrett stayed silent, standing in the darkness beside the shack.

'I received a message to come here,' Lambert called when he was thirty yards from Jarrett.

'I assume you're alone,' Jarrett said.

Lambert gave a sharp intake of breath and looked around until he identified where the speaker was standing. His nervous action helped to convince Jarrett that he wasn't planning anything duplicitous.

'I am.'

'Then I'm Jarrett Wade and I have a package from Ascott Beadley. He seemed to think you were expecting it.'

Lambert flinched at the mention of the lawyer's name and he lowered his head for several moments.

'I'd feared it was time for Ascott to contact me, and he chose the man to deliver the news well. I remember meeting you once, but that was a few years back. Why the secrecy for this meeting?'

'Because when I booked into your hotel I was being watched. I might not know what's interesting about the package, but I'd guess others do.'

Lambert glanced away. 'Quentin told me one of the rooms had been ransacked. Yours, I presume?'

'I assume it was, but I didn't wait around to find out what would happen.'

'That sounds a wise precaution. I had another robbery in the hotel five days ago. I got the feeling back then that the robber didn't find what he was looking for. It's possible you were expected.'

'I wasn't even hired five days ago. Then again, as this package has attracted a lot of interest, it's safe to assume someone would be hired to deliver it.' Jarrett shrugged. 'Either way, that's not my problem. If you can pay up, you can have the package, and we can part company.'

Lambert reached into his pocket and drew out an envelope.

'In that case, come out into the open and we can exchange packages.'

'I'd prefer to do this inside away from any prying eyes.'

Lambert glanced over his shoulder and back towards town.

'I don't reckon I was followed. On the other hand, I wasn't looking for anyone.'

Jarrett moved forward into the light and gestured for Lambert to follow him into the shack. Lambert thought about it, then dismounted.

Jarrett had reached the door when he heard a scraping sound. It might have been a night animal, but he flinched and looked around, seeking out the source of the noise.

Lambert noticed his concern and he stopped twenty yards from the doorway. Then he caught Jarrett's eye and pointed away from the railtracks towards the nearest stockyard.

Jarrett peered into the darkness; he discerned movement.

'Get inside quick,' he urged.

Lambert nodded and hurried on while Jarrett sidestepped through the doorway. He hunkered down in a position where he could peer outside.

Jarrett didn't see the movement again, but while Lambert ran he jerked his head around to look into the darkness; this time he looked in the opposite direction from where Jarrett had seen something.

A gunshot pealed out, the sound echoing, making it hard to work out where the shooter was. Lambert flinched and thrust his head down as he speeded up, but a second shot ripped out, making him screech.

Clasping a hand to his side, Lambert ran on for three paces until he stumbled and then fell full length.

Jarrett rose up and hurried out through the door, but a rapid volley of gunfire tore out and the dirt before his feet kicked as at least three slugs sliced into the ground.

He slid to a halt and, reckoning he would be more effective in being defensive, he fired wildly to either side while hurrying back to the shack. For his trouble, he was hurried on his way with retaliatory gunfire that made him run on for several paces through the door before he stopped.

He turned back. Thankfully, his intervention had given Lambert a chance. Lambert staggered to his feet, swayed, and then set off.

Jarrett ran back to the doorway where he urged Lambert on while firing blindly into the darkness, but Lambert managed only another two paces before two gunshots hammered into his chest from either side.

Lambert dropped to his knees and looked up at Jarrett.

'Run,' he mouthed.

Then he keeled over, to land face first in the dirt. Jarrett watched him, but Lambert didn't move again, so Jarrett patted the bulge in his pocket that he now wouldn't be able to deliver, before he turned his thoughts to his own survival.

The shack had a single window at the back and so wasting no time he hurried over to it. He cast a last look at the inert Lambert, then carried out his dying wish by rolling over the sill and dropping down into the darkness outside.

He knelt and listened. Aside from a few rustling sounds in the dark, he heard nothing. He moved away from the shack.

He reckoned the darkness that concealed Lambert's killers would also help him provided he edged along silently. The slope down to the tracks was ahead and although he didn't welcome the thought of clambering down it in the dark, he judged it to be a safer escape route than returning to the front of the shack.

He peered ahead, discerning the edge of the slope as a faint line between the dark ground at his feet and the lighter ground beyond the tracks. He was ten paces away from the edge when grit rustled to his right.

He kept moving, aiming to get closer to safety while avoiding revealing that he had heard the noise. He hoped the gunman would move again and reveal his exact location, but then a second footfall sounded. This time it was to his left, while a third set of footfalls sounded between him and the shack.

'So Jarrett Wade has returned to Hamilton to die,' a voice intoned in the dark from behind him.

The man must be confident of being in the superior position, or he wouldn't have divulged his exact location by speaking. Jarrett stopped and looked forward.

'Who are you?' he asked in a calm tone.

'You know.'

Three sets of footfalls sounded, each one advancing on him from a different direction, suggesting the speaker had given a signal. So Jarrett thrust his head down and ran for the edge.

He managed four paces before

gunfire ripped out.

Hot pain lanced down Jarrett's right arm, making him drop his gun and double over. He stumbled for a pace, then another gunshot tore into his left leg.

His legs buckled and he dropped to his knees, the action jarring his wounded leg and making him cry out for the first time.

The edge, offering potential safety, was only a few feet away, but it might as well have been 1,000 paces away, as he couldn't make his left leg work to get back up on his feet.

With one hand on the ground he crawled forward a mite, but that encouraged gunfire to rip out from either side. Slug after slug peppered into the ground between him and the edge, the loud whoops that accompanied each shot showing that the gunmen were enjoying themselves.

Jarrett continued to edge forward, every inch gained making his leg throb, and in response the shots got closer until the inevitable happened and lead sliced into his right leg.

The pain made Jarrett jerk upright on his knees before he wheeled round and, as he dropped, another shot hammered into his left arm. He crunched down on his back where he lay looking up at the stars.

The sight gave him comfort as dampness spread below him and his life blood poured out of him.

His right arm and leg lay over the edge of the slope, so he gritted his teeth and tried to move, but he was only able to twitch, confirming that he'd been shot in every limb.

The best he could do was to walk the fingers of his left hand along the lower ground, but he couldn't gain purchase to pull himself over the edge.

Then three men moved into his field of vision and looked down at him. He struggled to focus his eyes, but in the dark the men were no more than outlines.

'You look shot to hell, Jarrett,' the

leading man said.

Then he raised his gun, aimed down at Jarrett's chest, and fired.

* ★ ★

'What do you want?' Gerald Gough demanded.

'Information,' Ernest said, stomping to a halt before Gerald's desk.

'After you shot up Denby Grinnell I'm never giving you information again.'

Ernest tapped his chin, then walked around Gerald's office, taking note of his chipped and pitted desk, the crude and gaudy paintings on the wall, the well-worn poker table pushed into a corner.

Hill was familiar with the routine, so he admired an ornament, and then tested how hard he could poke it before it fell over. Gerald looked back and forth between the two men as he tried to work out which one of them would give him the most trouble.

'You know it doesn't work that way,' Ernest said. He scraped a finger along the frame of a painting and then appraised the dust he'd gathered. 'We've enjoyed a good working arrangement, except you violated it when you hid Denby.'

'I didn't violate anything. No matter what you claim, Denby didn't steal anything from Lambert Stevenson's hotel.'

'You make a good point.' Ernest stopped his pacing and bestowed upon Gerald a smile that made him sigh with relief. 'But there's been a second robbery.'

'That had nothing to do with me.'

'I never said it did, but you'll know who did it.'

Gerald shook his head. Then he reached into his top drawer and withdrew a handful of bills.

'This month's contribution to the law office funds is due by sundown tomorrow.' He waved the money. 'I thought you and I had an understanding, but I won't be paying you if you don't stop harassing me.'

'I decide how much leeway I give you and I decide how much you pay me for that leeway.'

Gerald shrugged. 'I always thought York Stevenson decided all the important things like how much leeway you gave me, who you arrested, when you went to sleep, when you wiped — '

'Enough! York is more important than you are, but I'm still the town marshal.'

'Of course you are.' Gerald fingered the bills, then, with a resigned shrug, slapped them down on his desk. 'So how much is this going to cost me?'

'An extra ten dollars a month.' Ernest waited until Gerald conceded his demand with a nod, then paced up to the desk. 'But it'll be a hundred if I don't get a name.'

Gerald's eyes flared, but when Hill moved forward to hover at his shoulder he spread his hands.

'I'll get you a name. I guess having robbers around doesn't do any of us no good.'

Ernest nodded to Hill and they backed away. With much smiling and mock pleasantry they left Gerald's office.

Then, for the sake of appearances, as it wouldn't help anyone if they were seen in the Wild Horse saloon too often, they slipped out through the back.

When they'd worked their way back to the main drag consternation was raging, with some people looking to the edge of town while others chatted and gestured boisterously. Hill beckoned the nearest man, Doc Cavanaugh, closer.

'There was a whole mess of shooting going on over there earlier tonight,' Cavanaugh said, pointing out of town down the railtracks. 'Apparently it sounded like a fearsome gunfight was going on.'

'It sounds like you might have yourself some business later.'

'And you,' Cavanaugh murmured, before Hill shooed him away.

The two lawmen looked out of town. Aside from the townsfolk debating what had been going on, all was silent now.

'A fearsome gunfight,' Ernest said.

'That sounds like a whole heap of trouble for someone,' Hill suggested.

Ernest nodded. 'I reckon that means it's time for some decisive action.'

'Agreed.'

The two men considered each other.

'In that case, coffee or whiskey?' Ernest asked.

Hill rocked his head from side to side.

'Coffee.'

Ernest nodded. Then they headed off in the opposite direction from the gunfire and back to the law office.

6

The stars twinkled down on Jarrett. They looked so bright and so close, Jarrett reckoned he could reach out and touch them, if only he could move.

He felt calm after his painful tumble down the slope, but he accepted that he only felt that way because he was so bullet-ridden he'd gone numb. He flexed his chest, wondering why he was still alive.

The gunman had stood over him and fired down at his chest, an act that had made Jarrett buck in pain so violently that he'd slipped over the edge and then down to the side of the tracks.

And yet the gunshot hadn't killed him.

His movement let him feel the weight on his chest and with a smile he realized that the slim metal case he had been unable to deliver to Lambert was still where he'd left it in an inside pocket. The case rested over his heart and it must have blocked the bullet.

His first piece of luck since he'd come out to the shack cheered him and he assessed the rest of the damage. It was as bad as he'd feared.

He had recalled what had happened correctly: he'd been shot in every limb.

The unseen gunmen had fired off dozens of wild shots to keep him from fleeing over the edge. So he assumed this had been a deliberate, ritual form of execution that should have culminated in a fatal shot to the chest.

He also recalled the gunman's last words to him, words that once he had been famous for using when he'd disposed of Orlando Pyle. He couldn't summon the energy to ponder on whether this could help him identify the gunmen.

'I sure have been shot to hell,' he murmured to himself.

As if someone had heard him speak, several faint voices sounded, but they were some distance above him. He assumed it was his would-be killer calling to the other gunmen, and he set about seeing if he could move.

He couldn't move his left arm or his right leg, but he could flex his right arm and his left leg, albeit with pain. So he pushed with the less wounded leg and clawed with his right hand, moving himself away from the voices.

Each action moved him for only a few inches, but he made progress and after the initial shouting he didn't hear anyone speak again. He didn't think he'd tumbled over the rail tracks, so he judged that moving away from the voice and the slope should move him towards the tracks.

By the time he'd pushed himself on for around fifty times, bolts of pain rippled down his left leg every time he moved, forcing him to rest. But then light glinted at his side, only feet away.

Two pushes later he saw the glint again and he was sure it came off the tracks; he confirmed this when his outstretched hand brushed cold metal.

He drew himself on to lie beside the tracks and face towards town. The shack that stood above him was a quarter-mile out of town and, afoot, it'd taken him only minutes to get here.

He figured it'd probably take him most of the night to return, if his strength held out.

He now felt strong enough to take stock of his condition more thoroughly. The leg that felt like a dead weight was drenched. He judged he'd be dead already if an artery had been hit, so he unhooked his belt and fashioned a tourniquet.

His left leg and arm weren't as damp and although he couldn't move the arm, he judged the damage to those limbs wasn't life threatening. The wound to his right arm was minor compared to the rest and his ribs throbbed, making him think one might be broken.

Feeling more confident now, he set off, lying on his side, dragging himself along the tracks with his hand and kicking against the sleepers with his foot. He made good progress for a while, passing ten sleepers before the pain in his leg forced him to stop.

He rested and then restarted. This time he managed five sleepers, the next time three, and the next two.

He resolved to cover one more sleeper and then rest; he managed this five times until he couldn't even move from one sleeper as far as the next before he had to rest. He lay with his forehead resting against the cold metal of the tracks and tried to work out how long this journey would take.

At this rate, he judged, he wouldn't even reach town by sunup. He would then have to trust his fate to luck: to someone venturing to that side of town and finding him before he faded away.

If he was going to get lucky, he was as likely to be lucky lying here as anywhere. He judged he would lose less blood and be more likely to be alive come sunup if he didn't move.

So he rested beside a sleeper and looked up at the stars, trying to judge how long he would have to wait for first light.

Voices sounded behind him and this time they were lower than before, suggesting the gunmen had found a way down. In the dark they would struggle to find where he had come to rest, never mind where he was now, but they might use the tracks to orient themselves, so he looked for a place to hide.

The slope loomed above him, a dark mass blocking out a large section of the night sky making the journey back feel even longer. He managed a clawed movement away from the tracks, but his strength gave out and he lay with his cheek pressed to the grit.

A pained cry sounded a hundred yards away followed by a thud, making Jarrett smile to himself despite his situation. Then other shouts went up as the rest of the gunmen tried to avoid falling too.

Heartened by their failure, Jarrett looked up and then winced. A man's form loomed up over him.

'Don't,' Jarrett murmured.

'I'm not here to harm you,' the man said, his voice gentler than the gunman's. He looked along the tracks towards the voices with consternation, confirming he wasn't one of the gunmen.

'Then help me.'

The man hunkered down beside him.

'Actually, I was hoping you'd help me,' he said.

* * *

'I've got good news and bad news,' Deputy Hill said when he arrived at the law office in the morning. 'Which one do you want to hear first?'

Ernest regarded his deputy without interest. For the last half-hour Saul Cox had been loitering around outside, presumably plucking up the courage to see him again, and his presence hadn't helped Ernest's sour mood.

'The bad news,' Ernest said.

'We've got a whole heap of new trouble to deal with. Lambert Stevenson has been killed.'

Ernest frowned. 'And the good news?'

'Lambert Stevenson has been killed.' Hill winked and waited for Ernest to snort a laugh. 'Do you want me to round up all the people who hated Lambert?'

'There's no need. We can congratulate them later.' Ernest saw that Saul was now heading across the main drag towards the office, so he put on a serious expression. 'Get all the details and ask around. See if anyone has any ideas about who did it.'

Hill noted where Ernest was looking and glanced over his shoulder. He saw Saul, then turned back to Ernest, his raised eyebrow inviting him to explain, but Ernest waved him away.

Hill left the office without complaint, although he did cast a long look at Saul before he moved out of view.

'It's later,' Saul said when he came in. 'Are you less busy now?'

'I've got a robbery to investigate and now a murder,' Ernest said.

'I'm sure you're on top of them.

Jarrett Wade says you're a fine and diligent man.'

'It's been a while since we last met.' Ernest sighed. 'So how do you know Jarrett?'

'I came to Hamilton with him.'

Surprise at this news countered Ernest's irritation and he leaned back in his chair to regard Saul with interest. He tapped his fingertips together as he appraised him and the young man returned his gaze without discomfiture.

'What do you want of me?' Ernest asked after a while.

'Nothing.' Saul shrugged. 'Although a few answers might help me before I decide what I want to do with my life.'

'Answers about what?'

'I never knew my father and when I asked my mother about him she refused to answer.'

Ernest frowned. 'I'm afraid I can't give you any answers either, because . . . because I don't know.'

'I feared that might be the case, but I'm sure the question has been a shock to you. I'll give you a few days to think some more. Maybe, before I move on, you might have remembered something that'll help me.'

'I might at that,' Ernest said, unable to suppress a smile at Saul's confident attitude. He waited until Saul started to turn away, then raised a hand. 'Where might I find you, if I remember anything?'

'I'm staying in the Wild Horse.'

Ernest winced. 'Gerald Gough is a low-down snake. The last outlaw I tracked down was holed up in one of his rooms.'

'That might be so, but the Wild Horse saloon is the cheapest place in town.'

Ernest opened his bottom drawer and withdrew half of the money he'd found in Denby Grinnell's house.

'Stay somewhere better.' He gestured with the bills to the north. 'Ma Hubbard keeps a clean establishment.'

'Obliged for the advice, but I'm not looking for charity.'

'Take it.'

Saul met his gaze. Then, with a quick smile, he took the money and left.

Ernest watched Saul leave until he was sure he was heading to the north of town. Then he turned his attention to the still open drawer.

A bottle of confiscated whiskey had rolled to the front. It was still early, but he picked up the bottle and found a glass.

'Why didn't you tell me, Malvina?' he asked, pouring himself a measure.

He leaned back in his chair and his gaze fell on the open drawer. The rest of the stolen money lying in there gave him one possible answer.

He knocked back the whiskey, then kicked the drawer shut.

7

A cool breeze wafted over Jarrett's face and for a moment he felt no different from how he felt on waking every morning.

A worrying thought tapped at his mind; but he batted it away and tried to hang on to the relaxed feeling, but he failed. So he took note of his surroundings, and to his surprise that made him relax again.

He was lying on a bed and, judging by the bandages and surgical instruments he could see on a nearby table, he was in a doctor's surgery.

'Is anybody there?' he croaked.

He waited, but nobody came, so he considered getting up. That didn't feel like something he wanted to attempt, so he looked up at the ceiling.

He must have dozed, as the next he knew was that someone was looking down at him. He had kindly eyes and he seemed pleased about something.

'I'm Doctor Cavanaugh,' the some-one said, 'and you're doing well.'

His voice was familiar and Jarrett realized that this was the man who had rescued him last night.

'Obliged for what you did,' Jarrett said. 'When you found me those gunmen were getting close.'

'I heard about the gunfire. Some others were heading out of town to investigate. I reckon they scared away whoever shot you up, so I can't take all the credit for that.' He smiled. 'But I can take plenty of credit for patching you up.'

'Will I live?'

'I hope so.' Cavanaugh winked. 'I have my professional reputation to think about.'

Jarrett mustered a snort of laughter.

'Quit with the putting me at ease routine and tell me the worst.'

'You already fear the worst, but I can tell you that you were lucky.'

'I know that, too. The gunmen tried

to wound me first to play with me, but they should have just finished me off when they had the chance.'

Cavanaugh nodded. 'That explains your wounds. Your left arm is broken, but the wound in your right forearm is minor. Your legs are both intact, but even after the stitching comes out you'll struggle to use them for a while. You may have broken a rib and you're weak from blood loss.'

'Were you seen bringing me here?'

'I've been dealing with gunshot wounds in Hamilton for fifteen years. I know when to be discreet.'

Jarrett cast his mind back. He couldn't remember this man from his last visit, but he detected from Cavanaugh's cautious answers that the doctor recognized him.

'You got any clue about who the gunmen are?'

'I have.'

Cavanaugh moved out of his view. Rattling sounded, then he returned clutching the small metal case. The seal was still in place and the case was intact, aside from the bullet hole in the top.

Jarrett cautiously moved his right arm to take the case. He turned it over to find a punched-out indentation where the slug had come to rest. Cavanaugh met his gaze and smiled before he moved away.

'Explain,' Jarrett called after him.

'You need to rest,' Cavanaugh called from the doorway. 'And to look after that case.'

Jarrett raised his head slightly. 'Is that the key to all this? Is that what the gun-men were after? Do you know what's in here?'

The questions exhausted Jarrett and he flopped back on the bed with the case resting on his chest. He thought Cavanaugh had left him, but after a few moments the doctor came back to the bed.

'I assume you won't rest easy until you get some answers.'

'Sure.'

Cavanaugh frowned, seemingly choosing his words carefully.

'I don't know what's in the case for sure, but bearing in mind the trouble it has caused, it's a reasonable guess that it concerns the ownership of Tyrone Hendrick's stockyard.'

'I didn't know it was in doubt.'

'It wasn't, but it could be now. Five years ago Tyrone put York Stevenson in charge while he left to enjoy his last years in peace. It's possible Tyrone has now died, or that he's decided who should inherit the yard. He didn't have any kin, so it's likely his good friend and York's brother Lambert was his choice.'

Jarrett raised the case and considered it, but even with the solution to the mystery only a wax seal away, he didn't want to violate his orders.

'And now?'

Cavanaugh shrugged. 'I'd expect the yard will go to someone else. That person may even be named in the document you don't want to look at.'

'And that person probably wanted the document, or at least wanted to stop Lambert from getting it. So if I open this up I might find out who gunned me down.'

'That's what I'd assume, but there's a simpler way to solve your mystery.' Cavanaugh smiled. 'You can ask me. I've been here since the early days and I know who Lambert trusted and who he didn't.'

'Three gunmen shot up Lambert and then me.'

Cavanaugh nodded. 'I know, and the first of those men is our deputy town marshal, Cornelius Hill.'

*　*　*

'Go away,' Ernest murmured, lying slumped over his desk. 'Leave me to die in peace.'

'After the amount of whiskey you drank yesterday,' Hill said, 'I doubt you'll feel peaceful for a while.'

Ernest agreed with this assessment

and he didn't complain when Hill slopped a coffee mug on his desk and then raised his head to ensure he sniffed the fumes. The coffee made Ernest's stomach lurch, but it also helped him regain enough of his senses to sit up.

'Did I spend the night here?'

'I tried to take you through to a cot in a cell to sleep it off, but you threatened to lock me in the jail-house if I moved you. So I left you.'

'Obliged, I suppose.'

Hill looked at him closely and Ernest could tell that his deputy was wondering whether to ask what was troubling him. As Ernest had acted oddly whenever Saul had come to see him, Hill would have figured out the cause of his anguish, but the marshal didn't reckon that sharing his problems would lessen them.

'You feel lively enough for a short ride?' Hill asked.

'Whatever's gone wrong now, you can deal with it.'

'Nothing new has gone wrong, but I reckon if you don't show an interest in what happened to Lambert Stevenson, it'll look odd.'

'That still troubling you?' Ernest sighed and, after gulping down the coffee, he got to his unsteady feet. 'I guess I ought to investigate this thoroughly before we find someone to blame.'

Once they were riding out of town the fresh air improved Ernest's spirits, although it didn't help his throbbing headache and the swaying didn't help his growing feeling of nausea.

When they arrived at the old shack the marshal let Hill take the lead in pointing out what he reckoned had happened, while he leaned against the wall with a hand to his head.

It seemed, according to Hill's terse summary, that Lambert had come out here and walked into an ambush. Several men had been involved.

'But I don't have no idea who did it or why,' Hill said, finishing off his explanation.

He looked at Ernest with the sly grin that he always adopted whenever he'd done the minimum he ought to do for the sake of appearances while he waited for confirmation that this would be enough.

It always had been before, but not today.

A mixture of the things Doc Cavanaugh had said to him recently, along with Saul's surprise appearance and memories of Malvina and the man he'd been back then had made Ernest restless.

He moved away from the house and stood over the bloodstains in the dirt. While turning on the spot, he tried to work out why Lambert had come out to this place in the dark.

'Came here or lured here?' he asked.

'Came,' Hill said with a shrug. 'Lambert's too cautious to be lured anywhere alone.'

'Perhaps he wasn't alone. He could have come here with his killer,' Ernest suggested. 'And his hotel was broken into twice by someone who was looking for something. Then Jarrett Wade arrived and disappeared.'

'Nobody's seen Jarrett since he booked the room that was then wrecked.'

'Which would suggest our first task is to find Jarrett.'

Hill laughed. 'And buy him a drink to celebrate.'

'No,' Ernest snapped, the loud retort making his vision lurch. He pressed a hand to his forehead until the swaying stopped. 'We find him so we can ask him if he knows who shot up Lambert.'

Hill looked at him with bemusement until, with a nod, he smiled.

'You're planning to investigate this properly because you're worried about what York will say.'

That wasn't Ernest's concern, but Hill thought it was and that saved Ernest from having to explain that after a night of heavy drinking and introspection, he'd got himself a conscience along with a sense of duty.

Although, when he thought about it, Hill was right and York was sure to have taken the news badly. While he wondered what York's response would be, he walked around the scene.

He found soft ground with footprints, from which he judged that three men had stood here, but they hadn't come close to where Lambert's body had been found.

He found more footprints behind the shack, but this time from only one person. He waved Hill over to offer an opinion, but Hill only shrugged, appearing bored with proceedings now that Ernest was showing every sign of investigating this murder properly.

With Hill mooching along behind him, Ernest examined the shack and then the surrounding area until he found dried bloodstains on rock behind the shack, along with more footprints from several people.

He doubted Lambert would have bled in two places that were so far apart, which meant another person could have been shot here.

'Wandering around here is just

wasting time,' Hill said. 'While you stare at the ground, Jarrett Wade is sure to be getting further away.'

'Then find him.' The marshal watched Hill frown, but the deputy said no more as he turned to his horse. 'And after you've got an answer about him, see Doc Cavanaugh and find out if anyone's been wounded recently. If he won't answer, pay him a bottle of whiskey, but no more.'

Hill grumbled at that and he trudged away leaving Ernest to continue examining the scene. The marshal found nothing else of interest, but he'd built up a better version of the events than Hill had given him.

He figured Lambert had come out here to meet someone, perhaps Jarrett, and he'd been attacked by three men. Lambert and someone else had been shot, but only one body had turned up.

This additional information cheered him. As he headed back to town he didn't even notice his headache, but that all changed when he found who was waiting for him in the law office.

York Stevenson was there, and he was sitting at Ernest's desk, his eyes pained and accusing.

Ernest sighed and headed inside to find that York had brought one of his three hired guns with him. The gun was loitering around the office adopting the same surly demeanour that he and Hill adopted whenever they visited Gerald Gough.

'Where are your other two guns?' Ernest asked.

'They're out searching for my brother's killer,' York said, while eyeing a discarded whiskey bottle with distaste. 'As you should be.'

'Rest assured that the investigation is proceeding quickly.'

'My only concern is that there has to be an investigation in the first place.'

'You can't blame me because someone killed Lambert.'

'You're the town marshal. It's your responsibility to foster a safe environment for the good people of Hamilton.

You've failed on that, just like you failed five years ago.'

'I can't change what happened back then, but right now I can find the people responsible for this crime and see that justice is served.'

York snorted. 'I care for legal justice as much as you do.'

Ernest nodded, the action making his head throb.

'Understood. I'll make whoever did it suffer.'

He turned away to look out of the window, and York stood up to join him. Ernest noted in the reflection that the hired gun stood behind him on the other side.

'Then stop drinking yourself senseless and act quickly. I have a fine reputation in this town as a man who keeps his word.' York gestured and his hired gun slapped a heavy hand on Ernest's shoulder, gripping it tightly. 'So trust me when I say this: don't fail me.'

8

Doctor Cavanaugh was talking to someone in the room next door. Jarrett couldn't force himself to concentrate on the conversation, but the voices were soft, so Jarrett didn't think it should concern him.

It took all his strength to keep his eyes open. He wasn't even sure how long he'd been lying here. With nothing to occupy his mind, he tried to cheer himself by planning what he'd do to the men who had shot him.

His acceptance that it'd be a while before he'd be strong enough to do anything tempered his enthusiasm, so he closed his eyes. To his irritation Cavanaugh came bustling in.

'I put him off by talking him up to two bottles of whiskey,' Cavanaugh said, 'but he'll back with them in a few minutes.'

Jarrett forced an eye open and considered Cavanaugh.

'Just go about your doctoring,' he said. 'I don't care about nothing right now.'

'You're not listening to what I said.' Cavanaugh pointed to the door. 'That was Deputy Hill.'

The name sounded familiar and, now that Cavanaugh had said it, Jarrett recalled that when the doctor had come in earlier, he'd told him that the deputy was at the door and that he'd try to get rid of him.

'It'd be best if nobody knows I'm here.' Jarrett yawned and closed his eye. 'But I trust you not to say anything.'

Cavanaugh shook his shoulder, forcing him to open both eyes.

'I know you're still weak and disoriented, but you have to concentrate. Hill is one of the men who shot you up.'

In a sudden moment of clarity Jarrett recalled the conversation he'd had with Cavanaugh, although he couldn't work out when he'd had it. It had involved the ownership of Tyrone Hendrick's stockyard and the men who had killed Lambert Stevenson to stop him inheriting it. Those men had included Hill.

If Cavanaugh had told him who the other two men were, Jarrett couldn't remember their names, but he remembered enough about this corrupt deputy.

'I'll make him regret the day he shot me and Lambert to hell,' Jarrett muttered. He moved to get up, but no matter how hard he strained, he stayed where he was. He sighed. 'Although that day won't be coming just yet.'

'Get up,' Cavanaugh urged. 'You won't get a better chance. Hill was asking about you. I stalled him, but he knows you're alive and he knows I'm a man who doesn't ask no questions when someone comes to me with a bullet wound.'

With his teeth gritted Jarrett raised his right arm and he used it to lay his splinted left arm across his chest. In this position he tried to twist himself on to his side, but he managed to rise for only a few inches before he flopped back down again.

'Then tell him you haven't seen me, or tell him you fixed me up and I left.' When Cavanaugh looked at him dubiously he waved vaguely with his right hand. 'Just tell him whatever lies you have to so he goes away.'

That speech exhausted Jarrett and he lay back down with his eyes closed. But Cavanaugh shook him again.

'Whatever else Hill is, he's a lawman. He won't just leave. He'll want to see my surgery and if I refuse, that'll just raise his suspicions.'

'What do you suggest I do? Perhaps I should lie here looking pitiful so he feels so much remorse for what he did that he shoots himself?'

Cavanaugh sneered. 'I'd heard you were a great bounty hunter. Perhaps I heard wrong.'

Jarrett knew Cavanaugh was only being harsh to goad him into acting, but it worked. With a supreme effort and a grunt of pain he rolled on to his side and then used his right elbow to lever himself up to a sitting position.

Jarrett felt precarious and in danger of toppling over, but Cavanaugh nodded with approval. He helped Jarrett to swing his legs round and place them on the floor.

Then Cavanaugh stood back, frowning.

'I'm willing to try,' Jarrett said. 'But I don't reckon there's any way I'm going to be able to stand up.'

'I wouldn't advise it either.'

Cavanaugh looked around as he put his mind to the problem; then, brightening, he scurried away. Jarrett's flash of anger was fading away and he was wondering how he could lie back down on the bed without hurting himself when Cavanaugh returned.

He was pushing a chair on wheels that creaked with every turn of the wheels. He left it in front of Jarrett and stood back to let him admire it.

Jarrett managed a begrudging nod.

'Provided you don't expect me to sneak up on Hill quietly and take him by surprise in that contraption, I reckon that'll let me move.'

Cavanaugh stood behind him. He slipped a hand under Jarrett's left armpit and encouraged him to put his right arm around his neck. Then they strained.

The first attempt failed to move him. The second effort made them both go sprawling on the bed, and while Jarrett was still cursing under his breath as the fall jolted his left arm, Cavanaugh rocked them both forward.

Jarrett tipped over and then twisted his hips. More by luck than judgement, he landed in the chair with such speed that the chair tipped over. Cavanaugh hurried round to the other side and jammed his feet against the wheels staying its progress.

Amid much creaking, and cursing from both of the men, the chair settled back down on both wheels, leaving Jarrett perched on the edge of its seat. Cavanaugh moved round to the front and pushed

Jarrett further into the chair.

'That went well,' Jarrett grunted, glaring up at Cavanaugh.

'It's progress,' Cavanaugh said. 'Now try moving.'

Jarrett lowered his right hand to the wheel and shoved. He didn't move. He sighed, rolled his shoulders and then strained harder.

This time he rolled backward for a few inches while the chair emitted a whining creak. The moment he stopped straining, it rolled back to where it'd been before.

Cavanaugh moved in to help, but Jarrett shooed him away. Despite the discomfort in getting here and the un-promisingly immobile feel of the chair, he reckoned he was better off sitting here than lying in the bed.

He slipped a hand under his right knee and moved the leg so that it was aimed directly forward. Then he repeated the operation with the other leg.

This new posture let him settle deeper into the chair. This time when he put a hand to the wheel he rolled backwards for a half-turn of the wheel before he had to rest and flex his arm.

He slumped back in the chair, his sudden burst of elation fading.

'I can move, but I don't reckon I'll be chasing after my would-be killers.'

'You don't need to do no chasing,' Cavanaugh said as, with excellent timing, the outside door opened.

Cavanaugh hurried over to the table beside Jarrett's bed and returned with his gun, which he dropped on to Jarrett's lap. He looked around the room, then settled for wheeling Jarrett to the wall behind the door.

Jarrett was too weak to object and he sat slumped in the chair without the energy even to keep his head up. Cavanaugh stood over him.

'Don't worry about me,' Jarrett murmured. 'You need to worry about getting all those bullets out of Deputy Hill.'

Cavanaugh drew an intake of breath suggesting his concern that Jarrett's show of bravado achieved the opposite effect to the one he'd intended, but he adopted a loud tone as he headed out of the surgery.

'You're back quickly,' he declared, 'Deputy Hill.'

'I've got no leads and Jarrett's trail isn't getting any warmer.'

'These two bottles should sure keep me and my patients warm, Deputy Hill.'

Jarrett winced, noting that despite talking loudly, Cavanaugh's comments sounded nervous.

'Talk first. Then you get the bottles.'

'Come through to my surgery, Deputy Hill, and I'll explain.'

Cavanaugh moved on and Jarrett could imagine Hill looking at Cavanaugh oddly and wondering why the doctor was repeatedly mentioning his name.

Strangely, the effect Cavanaugh had probably hoped to achieve worked. Jarrett raised his head, his anger at Cavanaugh's lack of subtlety overcoming his numerous pains.

He picked up the gun and, with his elbow resting on the side of the chair he aimed at a spot a few feet in from the door. He was behind the door and Cavanaugh didn't look his way as he came in.

Hill didn't follow him in immediately, making Jarrett grit his teeth as his gun hand began to tremble.

'I can see you had a patient,' Hill said from the doorway. 'Who was he?'

'He didn't give a name and I didn't ask for one, Deputy Hill, but he left this.'

Cavanaugh moved over to the bed, and this time Hill came in.

'What are you nervous about?'

Cavanaugh turned round with a benign smile on his face, but he made the mistake of glancing at Jarrett, which made Hill flinch and then swirl round. His gaze was high up and it took him a moment to lower his head to set eyes on Jarrett.

'Remember me?' Jarrett said. 'You shot me to hell.'

'Who are — ?'

Hill didn't get to finish his question

before Jarrett fired. Hill was standing only four feet away and Jarrett had aimed at the centre of his chest, but the slug only winged his arm.

The blow made Hill jerk backwards. Heartened by the memory of this man joining the other gunmen in repeatedly wounding him, Jarrett gathered enough strength to blast Hill low in the chest, making him double over.

A final shot through the top of his hat downed him. Then Jarrett flopped back in his chair and closed his eyes.

*   *   *

'How did you find him?' Ernest asked.

'I heard shooting behind the Wild Horse and went to investigate,' Doc Cavanaugh said. 'Hill was lying there. I'm sorry, but there was nothing I could do for him.'

'I can see that.'

Ernest stood over his deputy's body, not sure what he should feel. Hill had helped him dispense a kind of justice in Hamilton for the last five years, and their methods were sure to have annoyed many.

He had always presumed that, unless he kept his wits about him, this fate awaited him. Seeing his deputy receive it first made him wonder what mistake Hill had made.

'At least this gives you a reason to take on Gerald Gough now,' Cavanaugh said.

'It doesn't. Gerald wouldn't be behind this.'

Cavanaugh snorted. 'Gerald's tendrils have entwined their way into all the dirtiest cracks in Hamilton. I know you and he have an understanding, but without Hill around you're free to follow your instincts. Those instincts should tell you Gerald killed Lambert and now he's moved on to Deputy Hill.'

Ernest gazed upon Cavanaugh benignly. 'Those instincts tell me not to jump to conclusions, as you're doing.'

'I'm not. Lambert would have been even more successful without Gerald around.'

Cavanaugh noticed Ernest's sceptical look. 'Quentin Stone is Gerald's man in the Stevenson empire. If you won't question Gerald, question Quentin.'

Ernest frowned. He knew Cavanaugh was right but the fact that he'd never acted on that knowledge made him feel ashamed.

'Quentin is a little man, and I'm starting to think this is all connected to the biggest man of them all in Hamilton, York Stevenson.'

Cavanaugh looked at him with shock. 'Hamilton is prosperous only because of men like York. When we all worked at the stockyard, I doctored to him, and doctors get to know what makes a man tick. York is a decent man.'

'So they all say.' Ernest patted Cavanaugh's back. 'Now, leave me to do the investigating and I'll leave you to do the doctoring.'

'I'll do that, but don't forget what I told you before: remember who your friends are and you're sure to do the right thing.'

Ernest conceded the doctor's point with a smile and directed him to fetch the undertaker while he examined the scene. By the time the two men returned he had found nothing of interest. He headed back to the law office in a sombre mood.

That mood didn't lighten when he'd been at his desk for an hour and had started work on another bottle of confiscated whiskey.

After York Stevenson had threatened him Ernest had been sure that York knew more about his brother's death than he'd let on, but he struggled to make a connection between York and Hill. Worse, he had become used to having Hill around to share ideas with, even if they had rarely been about the crimes they were supposed to be investigating.

That thought led him to think that, as they had been investigating Lambert's death properly, Hill might have stumbled across an answer and had paid the price. Ernest put the bottle away and walked over to the window.

The stockyards could be seen from everywhere in town. Although the Wild Horse blocked most of his view of York's yard, the largest and the first to be built here, he could still see the cabin from where York presided over his domain in Tyrone's absence.

Cavanaugh had urged the marshal to follow his instincts and the doctor was convinced that that would lead him to Gerald Gough. Ernest didn't agree.

Quentin Stone might be Gerald's man in the Stevenson empire, but Quentin wasn't averse to selling information to whoever paid him. More importantly, Ernest reckoned that events during Hamilton's early days governed what was happening now.

Once, when this town had been nothing more than a huddle of clapboard buildings and the railroad had been just a dream, Tyrone Hendrick had opened the first stockyard. He had trusted the running of the yard to three men: Ernest, and the Stevenson brothers York and Lambert.

There had been others around who were still in town, like Gerald Gough, Doc Cavanaugh and, until recently, the now deceased Cornelius Hill, but these three had been in the positions of power. In their various ways, they had all vied for Tyrone's attention.

Ernest had looked after the workers. He had resolved their disputes and later he had protected the yard's growing riches from anyone who might want to take them.

York was a former rancher, so the cattleman had devoted himself to the logistics of the operation.

Lambert had been Tyrone's deputy. He was as astute a businessman as Tyrone was and he had immersed himself in every aspect of the business.

Tyrone having no kin, he had made it obvious that he'd pass on the ownership of the stockyard to a business associate. Everyone had assumed that that man would be Lambert, yet he never appeared pleased at the prospect of having that honour bestowed upon him.

Lambert would have been successful no matter what he'd turned his hand to, and he didn't view inheriting the stockyard as being an important goal.

It had appeared that nothing could stop the yard's success, but then the trouble started. Orlando Pyle and his bandit gang had preyed on the stockyard and Ernest couldn't stop them, no matter how many guns he hired.

With every raid Ernest's reputation diminished in Tyrone's eyes, and he was on the verge of being replaced when he had a spot of luck. Jarrett Wade ended Orlando's reign of terror and although Tyrone was delighted, it initiated a change.

The prolonged disruption had destroyed the ageing Tyrone's enthusiasm and he announced that he'd retire to live his last days enjoying the fruits of his labours. He had to choose a successor from a security man with a tarnished reputation, a cattleman with little business acumen, and a businessman with an impeccable record.

Ernest hadn't expected to be chosen

and York had also assumed he wouldn't be picked, but Tyrone had decided he wanted a cattleman to preside at the head of his empire. He left York in charge, although he made it clear that he hadn't decided yet who would inherit.

York judged that he was being tested, and in the months after his appointment he operated a ruthless regime that tested everyone's patience. Before long Ernest and Lambert both left the yard.

New stockyards were being built and Hamilton was growing. As Gerald Gough was prospering by providing basic entertainment for the workforce, Lambert judged he could make his fortune, too. He built hotels and saloons and he prospered.

Ernest became Hamilton's first town marshal. Whether he had prospered was open to debate.

Now, five years on, Lambert had been killed, presumably to stop him inheriting the stockyard. Hill had perhaps worked some of this out, and he had been killed.

York had given the marshal an

ultimatum to find Lambert's killer, but Ernest reckoned this could be a distraction to stop him thinking about who had the most to gain from Lambert's demise. He did not need to ponder on the fact that if his theory was right, he might also be viewed as someone who could inherit the yard and so could be the next to be killed.

He stepped outside and, without a clear plan in mind, he walked down the main drag until he fetched up at Ma Hubbard's. Saul was sitting by the window with a bored expression that changed to a hopeful smile when he saw Ernest.

Ernest wasn't used to anyone being pleased to see him, and he sloped inside uncertainly.

'Have you remembered something that might help me?' Saul asked.

Ernest had tried to avoid thinking about Saul's mother and about what that implied.

'I haven't. I've been busy and I'm about to get even busier, but I've been thinking that your mother was a good friend. I owe her plenty. You seem a sensible young man, so I thought I could offer you a job.'

Saul raised an eyebrow. 'As your deputy?'

'That would be a dangerous position for one so young, but I could do with someone to keep the office tidy, take queries when I'm not there, and so forth.'

Saul frowned. 'I'm my own man and I'll take no favours — '

'I hear what you're saying, but sitting staring out of the window and looking bored in the law office while getting paid has got to be better than just sitting here looking bored.'

'You make a good point. When can I start?'

'You already have.'

Ernest turned to the door. Saul scurried after him. As they walked back down the main drag Saul glanced at the marshal several times, clearly wondering whether to question him; Ernest was pleased that he didn't.

At the office he explained Saul's duties, then turned to leave.

'That all doesn't seem too difficult,' Saul called after him. 'Maybe when I've proved myself, you might want me to do more and be your deputy?'

Ernest stopped in the doorway and looked up at York's cabin, high up in the stockyard.

'You're your own man,' he said. 'You wouldn't want to do that.'

9

'How are you feeling today?' Cavanaugh asked, peering down at Jarrett's bed.

'No different from yesterday,' Jarrett said with pained and narrowed eyes. 'I feel like I got shot to pieces and you put me back together again.'

'Which is what I did.' Cavanaugh smiled. 'Except I'm sure you feel better than Deputy Hill does.'

Jarrett nodded and moved to raise himself on to his good elbow. To his delight, unlike yesterday, he completed the movement without too much difficulty.

'Has anyone asked any questions about him?'

'I left the body behind the Wild Horse saloon and then fetched Marshal Montague. Ernest asked plenty of questions, but I told him a story that he believed.' Cavanaugh smiled. 'Nobody suspects you're even here, never mind that you killed him.'

'Except Hill's fellow would-be killers will suspect plenty and they're sure to come looking for me before long.'

'I know, and that's why you have to act quickly.'

Jarrett winced. 'I was afraid you'd say that, but unless you can entice the other gunmen here for me to kill, I can't see me being able to do anything.'

Cavanaugh moved away and returned with the wheeled chair.

'You have an opportunity now, and it's too good to miss.'

Jarrett eyed the chair with irritation.

'Is this opportunity the only chance I'll get?'

'No, I'll have to — '

'Then I'll miss it.' Jarrett flopped back down on the bed. 'Revenge can wait until I can move.'

'I've made the chair quieter.' Cavanaugh pushed the chair back and forth, producing a series of squeaks that didn't sound much quieter than they had done yesterday.

'I don't care. I need to rest.'

Cavanaugh took his shoulder and dragged him up to a sitting position.

'Lying there is the worst way of getting yourself fit again.'

Jarrett registered Cavanaugh's firm gaze that suggested the doctor wouldn't relent until Jarrett did his bidding. He sighed and held out a hand. Cavanaugh moved the chair closer.

With greater ease and skill than yesterday, Jarrett managed to swing off the bed and into the chair. He shuffled back into the position he'd found most comfortable yesterday, but he still sat slumped and glaring at Cavanaugh.

'Who next?' he asked.

'Gerald Gough, the owner of the Wild Horse saloon. It's beside the surgery.'

'I remember Gerald from the last time I was here. I had a few drinks in his saloon, and he was a sociable and popular man. He didn't seem the sort of man who'd shoot me up.'

'Any man is that sort of man if some-one is standing between him and owning the largest stockyard in Hamilton.'

Jarrett nodded. 'Who was the third man at the shack that night?'

Cavanaugh winked. 'Only when you've taken care of Gerald.'

Jarrett felt too sore and weak to argue the point, especially when he had to conserve his strength for the task ahead.

'How will I take advantage of this opportunity?' he asked when Cavanaugh had handed over his gun.

'I see Gerald on the first Monday of every month. Nobody else knows I see him, so nobody will be around. This time I'll have company.'

'What do you see him about?'

Cavanaugh winked. 'As you said, Gerald is a sociable and popular man.'

Cavanaugh waited until Jarrett nodded his understanding, then he collected his black bag. He dropped it on Jarrett's lap on top of the gun. Then he turned the chair to the back door and wheeled him on.

Cavanaugh moved Jarrett with greater ease than Jarrett was able to move himself, so by the time they'd reached the back door some of Jarrett's misgivings had receded. He propped his splinted left arm against the bag while he kept Cavanaugh's bag from moving with his right hand.

Once they were outside they moved over soft dirt, but when they reached an expanse of rough ground every jolt made pains shoot up and down both of Jarrett's legs. Thankfully, the journey only took a minute, but by the time Cavanaugh stopped pushing the chair Jarrett's fragile good mood had eroded and his stomach churned with nausea.

'We need to wait,' he murmured.

Cavanaugh moved round to look down at him.

'You look fine,' he said. 'Revenge will get your blood pumping like it did yesterday.'

'Except this doesn't sit well with me. I've never been one to harbour thoughts of revenge.'

'You've never been shot up by three gunslingers before.'

'I haven't, but I'm sure it wasn't personal.'

Jarrett thought for a moment or two, and now that he'd voiced his mind he accepted that Cavanaugh was right. He had only ever gone after men for bounty, not to resolve personal vendettas, but these men had gone after him because he stood in the way of their aims. Again, it hadn't been personal.

'Except if you don't make them pay, they're sure to come for you because you still have the contract that details who will inherit the stockyard,' Cavanaugh pointed out.

Jarrett patted his pocket, feeling the bulge that had saved his life and accepting that he still had a job to complete, even if he didn't know whom he needed to give this document to now. He nodded. Cavanaugh turned the chair round and wheeled him backwards into the back of the saloon.

As they headed down a corridor Cavanaugh slowed down to a pace that Jarrett could have managed on his own, limiting the noise the chair made to a pained screech with every turn of the wheels. At a corner Cavanaugh stopped and looked down the next corridor before moving on to a door.

'What now?' Jarrett murmured, struggling to keep his eyes open as Cavanaugh positioned him before the door so he could be moved inside quickly.

'Rest up and gather your strength,' Cavanaugh whispered. 'I'll fetch you when Gerald is distracted.'

Cavanaugh removed the bag from Jarrett's lap and tapped on the door three times. He waited for a hushed reply, then slipped inside.

Gerald said something to Cavanaugh and Cavanaugh replied calmly. As the doctor wasn't acting as nervously as he had done with Hill, Jarrett settled down.

For several heartbeats he fought to keep his eyelids open, then he let tiredness win. He reckoned he must have dozed, as a nearby noise made him come to his senses with a start.

People were approaching. They were coming down the next corridor and closing on the corner ten feet away.

'I don't know what that squeaking noise was,' a man said.

'Whatever it was, we should ignore it,' another man said. 'This is the morning when Doctor Cavanaugh makes his secret calls.'

The first man laughed, but they still walked on. When Jarrett was sure they wouldn't stop before they turned the corner and saw him, he put a hand to the wheel and moved on.

Spurred on by concern about his imminent discovery, he spun the wheel with greater strength than he'd managed before; the chair rolled into the door and knocked it open. Cavanaugh must have left the door slightly ajar as the collision didn't slow Jarrett down and he rolled on into the room.

He gave the wheel another twirl as he looked around for Gerald and Cavanaugh, finding them by the wall. Cavanaugh was in the process of removing a bottle from his bag while Gerald was sitting on a table and loosening his clothing.

'What's the meaning of this?' Gerald

demanded, standing up hurriedly.

'You shot me to hell,' Jarrett said. He felt around for the gun on his lap, his weakness and befuddled senses causing him to locate it only on the third attempt. Then he raised the gun, the effort taking all his concentration. 'But you should have finished the job.'

'But who in tarnation are — ?'

Gerald didn't get to complete the question before Jarrett fired, hammering a slug into the centre of his chest, downing him. Gerald had been to his right and Jarrett found it easier to move in that direction, but he still smiled at his success in dispatching Gerald in a less sloppy manner than he'd killed Hill.

While he watched Gerald settle on the floor and then lie still, rapid footfalls sounded behind him. The two men came in through the door. They stopped behind his chair and Jarrett struggled to turn to face them.

A grunt of anger sounded and one man hurried to Gerald while the other man grabbed the chair from behind and tipped it forward, spilling Jarrett to the floor. His legs being stiff, Jarrett could do nothing to stop himself and he fell forwards.

At the last moment he managed to lower his right elbow and that hit the floor first, limiting some of the impact, but he still lay on the floor floundering as pains cramped both legs.

'Gerald's dead,' one of the newcomers said.

'I thought you were looking after him,' the other man said to the doctor.

'I was,' Cavanaugh whined, 'but that man came bursting in and he shot Gerald up.'

A snort sounded and one of the men moved over to Jarrett.

'He doesn't look capable of bursting in anywhere,' the man said. 'But keep a gun on him. I'll see who it is.'

The man slapped a hand on Jarrett's back and dragged him up to a hunched position. Jarrett didn't resist, and the man bent down and put two hands to the task of rolling him over.

Jarrett landed on his back, the jarring thud making his legs feel as if someone had set fire to them. He couldn't focus through his watering eyes, but he saw the blurred image of the man standing over him. He raised himself slightly while jerking his gun up.

He fired. The blast made the man cry out. Then the man fell away, clutching his chest, while for Jarrett the effort involved in keeping himself raised proved too great and he crashed down on his back.

The second man fired. The slug sliced into the floor above Jarrett's shoulder. Jarrett presumed that his own sudden movement had saved him, but he was beyond being able to do anything in retaliation as the pain in his legs coursed up to his chest and then into his arms.

His gun arm clattered down on the floor as he lay spread-eagled, presenting an easy target, but the gunman didn't take advantage. Jarrett blinked rapidly. When his vision focused he saw that

Cavanaugh and the other man were struggling.

Cavanaugh was being ineffectual: he was holding his opponent's gun arm with two hands as he tried to keep the gun away from him. His opponent sneered with confidence and shoved him away, sending Cavanaugh falling on to his back.

The gunman followed Cavanaugh with his gun, but Jarrett made him pay for his mistake in not taking him first when, with his teeth gritted, he levered up his arm and sliced a shot into the gunman's side. The man dropped to his knees; this moved him closer, letting Jarrett dispatch him with a deadly shot to the head.

Then Jarrett flopped down. He didn't reckon he would be able to raise the gun again, no matter who threatened him. Cavanaugh scurried around checking on the men.

His satisfied grunts told Jarrett they'd get no more trouble from them. Then he righted the chair.

'That was messy,' he said. 'We need

to get out of here quickly.'

'Gerald didn't remember me,' Jarrett murmured. 'He ought to know the man he tried to kill.'

'He must have been surprised you were still alive,' Cavanaugh said, putting Jarrett's right arm over his shoulder. 'Now hold on and we'll get you in the chair.'

Jarrett was too weak to keep his arm in place and it flopped back down on the floor with a thud. Cavanaugh put his hands under his back and raised him.

Jarrett felt something in his left leg tear. Then he lost all interest in asking more questions.

10

'I told you to stay outside,' Ernest said.

'Actually,' Saul said, 'you told me to stay back in the law office.'

Ernest glanced at Saul sternly, but when the young man only smiled, he stood back and with a mock bow invited him to come into Gerald Gough's office.

He expected that the sight inside would shock Saul, who would then make a hasty departure and afterwards not ignore his orders again, but the young man regarded the three bodies with calm detachment.

He walked around Gerald's body, nodded, then moved on to stand over the other men. He looked from the bodies to the door and back again, then grunted to himself.

'What do you reckon?' Ernest asked.

'I reckon Gerald knew his killer, but something unexpected happened such as an argument that escalated into a gunfight. The other men came rushing in and they got shot for their trouble.'

'Why do you think that?'

'Gerald's shirt buttons are undone, as if he were changing clothes, which he wouldn't do unless he knew his visitor, and the other men look like they've fallen after running to help Gerald.' Saul shrugged. 'Or at least, that's what it looks like to me.'

Ernest hadn't noticed any of these details, but then, until recently the complexities of investigating crimes properly had never concerned him and Hill.

When someone had committed a crime he and Hill had found someone and made them suffer. It had never mattered to them if the first someone was connected to the second someone.

'Obliged for your opinion,' Ernest said.

Saul frowned. 'I guess that all sounded too simple to a lawman like you. How will you work this out?'

Ernest moved past the bodies and stood at the window, looking up at York's cabin on the edge of the stockyard.

'I tend to look out of the window and wait until I see the guilty person.'

'I don't understand.' Saul waited, but Ernest said nothing more, so Saul pointed at the door.

'I should go back to the law office and do what you told me to do.'

Ernest turned from the window and offered Saul a friendly smile.

'Do that, but make sure you keep on giving me your opinion.' Ernest winked. 'But only when I ask for it.'

Saul smiled before he left the room, leaving Ernest to pace around considering the scene. No ideas would come, so he turned back to the window to survey the stockyard.

He had thought York would come for him next, but he had gone for Gerald, even though Gerald was unlikely to inherit the yard.

Perhaps York needed him, Ernest, alive to bolster the illusion that he wasn't involved, or perhaps the doctor had been right all along and Gerald *had* been involved in recent events.

Whatever the answer, York had clearly distanced himself from the events. York had three hired guns and three men had been at the shack where Lambert had been killed.

Now three men had been killed in a gunfight and all this suggested that York was eliminating his potential rivals.

With that matter resolved in his own mind, Ernest stepped outside. He moved round to the front of the saloon, from where he could see into the law office.

Saul was sweeping up, and Ernest had no doubt he would do a good job minding the office while he was gone, no matter for how long that might be. Then he turned and walked over to his horse.

He mounted and rode off on the short journey to the stockyard.

* * *

'Leave me alone,' Jarrett muttered.

Cavanaugh shook his arm again and held out a bowl brimming with steaming broth.

'You need to eat this to regain your strength,' he said with a kindly smile.

'I'm not killing anyone else today.'

'I'm not asking you to. You hurt your leg during your earlier tumble. I've put a fresh bandage on the wound and it should be fine, but you need to concentrate on recuperating.' Cavanaugh chuckled. 'Anyhow, I gather the last of your would-be assassins is still busy right now. He's sorting out the mess in that room in the Stevenson hotel that you never got to sleep in.'

Jarrett considered the bowl and shook his head.

'Who is he?'

'That's not important right — '

'Tell me.'

'Quentin Stone.' Cavanaugh waited, but Jarrett didn't react. 'Quentin is Gerald's man in the Stevenson empire, and he's the meanest varmint of them all. He's probably the man who tried to finish you off.'

Jarrett nodded and levered himself up on to an elbow to accept the soup.

From the bowl placed on the bed at his side he spooned the broth slowly to his mouth while thinking rapidly.

Quentin had attended the desk in the hotel when he'd walked in, then he'd scurried outside to tell three other men that he'd arrived. He was clearly a snake, but he was a man who ran errands for others, not a ruthless gun-toting killer.

Most important, the man who had tried to kill him had taunted him, and that man hadn't sounded like Quentin, or for that matter Gerald or Deputy Hill. Neither had Hill or Gerald showed any sign that they'd recognized him.

Cavanaugh looked at him oddly, as if he'd detected what was concerning him, so Jarrett smiled until he moved away.

When Cavanaugh had left the surgery Jarrett waited for a moment in case he looked back in, then he drew the small metal case out of his inside pocket.

He had taken this job with the instruction that he must not open the case. Despite everything that had happened, he balked at the thought of violating that instruction. He glanced again at the closed door, then prised away the seal.

The folded document was inside, and the flattened slug that had nearly killed him was embedded in the centre of the papers. Jarrett drew the slug out and considered it.

With a smile he slipped the bullet into a pocket, then flicked open the document. He began reading.

The arcane legalistic terms, designed to leave the document's intent in no doubt made him struggle to work out what that intent was. So he returned to eating the broth while reading the document from the start, one tortuous sentence at a time.

As Cavanaugh had thought, it did concern the ownership of the stockyard and Lambert Stevenson was Tyrone Hendrick's chosen successor, but there were provisions and limitations that made Jarrett's fragile mind spin.

When he heard Cavanaugh moving in the next room he wasn't disappointed that he could postpone trying to understand the legalities until later.

He slipped the document back in its case and tucked it into his pocket. Then he finished off the broth.

'Obliged for the broth,' Jarrett called out when Cavanaugh came in. 'I sure feel stronger now.'

'Then I'm pleased,' Cavanaugh said as he took the bowl. 'I'll start working on a plan to get Quentin Stone alone so you can complete your revenge.'

'Do that, but not too quickly.' Jarrett lay back down on the bed with a groan. 'Hopefully, by the time you've come up with a plan I'll be fit enough to listen to your explanation of how Quentin, Gerald and Deputy Hill wanted to stop Lambert getting the stockyard.'

Cavanaugh shrugged. 'I'm not sure I understand it either.'

'That's what I feared, so I don't want to kill Quentin before I find out why he shot me to hell. So we need to take Quentin alive and question him.'

'You can't take any chances.'

'This is my revenge and that means

it's my chance to take.' Jarrett eyed the aggrieved-looking Cavanaugh. 'You're just helping me and I'm obliged for that, but I want to wait until I'm stronger.'

Cavanaugh turned away to the table at the side of the room, where he kept Jarrett's gun. He busied himself with tidying away bottles and Jarrett settled down.

After eating he felt tired and ready to doze, but he managed to keep an eye cracked open.

Presently Cavanaugh glanced his way, then slipped Jarrett's gun under his jacket and moved towards the door. Jarrett didn't react, but at the door Cavanaugh stopped and glanced at him. Jarrett closed his eyes.

Cavanaugh muttered something under his breath, proving that Jarrett had not been quick enough. Then he moved over to him.

'What's worrying you?' he asked.

Jarrett struggled to open his eyes; when he'd managed to half-open them he delivered a long yawn. He avoided looking at the bulge under Cavanaugh's jacket.

'Deputy Hill and Gerald Gough didn't recognize me. I'd expect that the two men who had shot me up would remember me.'

'When they shot you it was dark.'

'It was, but I met Quentin. He's no gun-toting killer. The three men whom Quentin spoke to outside the hotel are probably the actual gunmen.'

'You're mistaken.'

'I only have your word for that and from where I'm lying it looks to me like I've been enacting your revenge against men you hate, not mine.'

'I'd heard you were an astute man. Even when shot to hell, clearly you've kept your keen mind.'

Jarrett didn't feel astute right now and he yawned again.

'Why?'

'For the last five years I've urged Ernest Montague to face up to the men who are holding him and Hamilton back, the cruel men like Cornelius Hill, the corrupt men like Gerald Gough and the snakes like Quentin Stone. He's ignored me, but let us hope that the start we've made in cleaning up this town will turn him in the right direction.'

'I knew Ernest. He was a good man.'

'He was and he's still a trusted friend. I reckon the man he used to be is still in there somewhere, but he's yet to claw his way out from under all the people who are holding him back.'

'You may be right, but even from the little I've learnt, I reckon York Stevenson has the most to gain from Lambert's death.'

'He has, but York wouldn't kill his own kin.'

Jarrett could still concentrate enough to keep sleep at bay, and he glared at Cavanaugh.

'It seems to me that you've worked out some of the wrongs in this town, but you haven't got the ability to unearth them all. You're a doctor. You're not a lawman or a manhunter and you'd be best served by concentrating on your doctoring and leaving such matters to those who understand them.'

'I have done, but every year I've seen Ernest slipping further into the mire. He lost respect when he couldn't stop Orlando Pyle and he's never got it back. I had to do something and we're nudging him in the right direction.'

Cavanaugh smiled and removed the gun from under his jacket. Jarrett looked at the gun, but the fact that Cavanaugh had taken it no longer felt important.

'I assume,' he said, his voice sounding odd to his ears as if he were speaking slowly at the bottom of a barrel, 'you're about to threaten me to do your bidding.'

'You assumed right, but not with this gun. If I was confident with weapons, I'd have killed those men myself, but I need you to do it.'

'Except now I won't.'

Jarrett closed his eyes, so Cavanaugh poked his sore rib until he opened them again.

'I can employ other methods. They're

ones that would have drawn attention to me if I'd tried them on Hill and Gerald, but it won't concern anyone when I use them on a man nobody knows is here.'

'I don't . . . I don't give in to no threats,' Jarrett said, although he wasn't sure that those words emerged, as his voice was slurred and his mouth would no longer work, so that drool was dribbling down his chin.

'That's no threat. I've already started. That broth you enjoyed contained a bromide. I'm sure you can feel its effects already, and now you couldn't move even if you were fit. From now on I'll keep you sedated.'

'Not killing nobody,' Jarrett mumbled around a yawn.

'Except you will. I have instruments in here that can remove bullets, but they can cause harm, too.' Cavanaugh glanced around the room, then smiled down at Jarrett. 'I'll leave you to think about that. When I return, I'm sure you'll give me a different answer.'

Jarrett tried to reach up and slap Cavanaugh's face, but his arm felt leaden and he couldn't raise it. In spite of himself his eyes closed, and this time they stayed closed.

11

Ernest dismounted outside York's cabin.

Through the window he could see that only York was within, sitting at his desk, so he headed inside.

York glanced up and considered him with disdain before he returned to writing in a large ledger.

'I hope you're not here to make excuses,' he said. 'I only want to see you when you have good news.'

'I have news, but then again it won't be news to you.'

York sighed and pushed the ledger away from him.

'Stop talking in riddles and get to the point.'

'If you want plain speaking, Gerald Gough is dead.'

York frowned and leaned back in his chair, his subdued reaction giving the impression that he hadn't known.

'I won't say that I'm saddened by this news and it won't change my ultimatum to you. I care only about you finding the man who killed my brother.'

'Except I believe that the man who killed Gough and the killer of your brother is the same man, and I know who that man is.'

York smiled and gestured for him to approach his desk. Ernest noted that he used the movement to hide his glancing outside.

'Then don't keep your good news a secret any longer.'

'I believe this is all to do with the ownership of the stockyard. Tyrone Hendrick has nobody to pass the business on to and, of the three people he trusted the most, he chose your brother. With Lambert dead, that left two candidates. Gerald's death reduces the choice still further.'

'Are you telling me that the killer's motive was to get his hands on this stockyard?'

Ernest reckoned that York was asking

questions rather than giving answers in order to lengthen this meeting and so let whoever he'd signalled to outside get word out that he had a problem, but he didn't mind. He hadn't expected to leave the stockyard with York under arrest without confronting York's hired guns.

His only hope of surviving the next few minutes rested on York being unprepared to act openly when so many people would have seen him come in.

'That would be my assumption,' Ernest said.

York tapped his fingertips together. 'Is that your way of telling me that you're the killer?'

Ernest smiled. 'No.'

'But that leaves only me.' York put a hand to his chest in apparent indignation. 'Surely you can't suspect that I'd kill my only brother to ensure my ownership of a business that I've run for the last five years and which Lambert had no chance of acquiring?'

'We all know Tyrone let you run this

place as a test. Perhaps you've failed and he's decided to let a businessman run it and not a cattleman.'

'This place is a success.'

'It is, but then again it was a success before Tyrone left and its continued success has little to do with you. Tyrone built this place from nothing and Lambert had proved his worth by building an empire for himself from nothing, too.'

Shuffling sounded outside the door behind Ernest's back, making York smile with confidence.

'That's an interesting theory. Do you have proof?'

'I don't have the time to explain it now that your three hired guns are standing behind that door waiting for your order to come in.'

'Actually there's only one man, Dexter Pyle. The other two guns are out searching for Lambert's killer.'

'They don't need to search far. Three men were at the shack where Lambert was killed, and three men were killed in the Wild Horse saloon.'

York raised an eyebrow and since Ernest said nothing more, Ernest couldn't blame him for smirking.

'Is that tenuous connection all you have?'

'For now, and it's enough for me to arrest you while I work out the rest.'

York sneered. 'What can someone like you possibly work out?'

Ernest placed his hands on the desk and leaned forward.

'We both know there was a witness to Lambert's murder. He was wounded, but he got away and your hired guns haven't found him yet. I intend to find him first and I'll be interested to hear what he has to say.'

York met Ernest's eye, but he gulped and that was enough to confirm to Ernest that he had deduced the situation correctly. He backed away to keep both York and the door in view.

'Dead men can do no harm,' York said, standing up.

His action appeared to be a signal, as the door swung open and his hired gun marched inside to take up a position beside the door.

'I reckon Jarrett Wade is still alive.'

York took a moment before he moved around the desk, his pause confirming to Ernest that he had worked out another aspect of what was happening.

'I didn't mean Jarrett,' York said as he stood before him. 'I meant you.'

'There's no need for more threats. I'm only accusing you as I'm entitled to, seeing as how I'm the town marshal.'

'In that case, I have the right to answer your accusation. I didn't kill Gerald. I didn't even know he was dead until you told me. I had no reason to want him dead and even if I accept your theory that I'm eliminating men who might inherit the stockyard, I wouldn't expect Gerald to have been considered as a likely owner, as you did.'

Ernest shrugged. 'I'm inclined to believe you about that.'

'I didn't kill my brother either.' York raised a hand when Ernest sneered. 'Or at least I didn't pull the trigger. Dexter

Pyle over there did that.'

York flicked his gaze to the door where the hired gun tipped his hat in salute, forcing Ernest to move so that he could watch Dexter.

'Orlando Pyle's brother?'

'Sure,' Dexter said.

'Why would . . . ?' Ernest swirled round to face York. 'All the trouble that happened here five years ago nearly ruined my career and it wore Tyrone down so much he retired. I could never stop Orlando's activities, but that's only because you were behind them!'

York clapped his hands slowly. 'It's taken you five years, but Hamilton's trusty town marshal has finally solved his first case.'

'And that's when it all started going wrong for me. I lost the respect of the townsfolk and I never got it back.'

He didn't need to add that this was when he'd lost respect for himself but York smirked, as if he already knew this.

'So does this make you feel worthy of the position now?'

Ernest paused for a moment to emphasize his answer.

'It does.'

York matched Ernest's confident smile, then snorted a laugh.

'Then it's a pity that it'll be your last success.'

York flicked a glance at Dexter, but Ernest had already anticipated that action. He grabbed York's arm and tugged. By the time Dexter had drawn his gun and levelled it on him, Ernest was standing behind York and had wrapped an arm around his neck.

He jabbed his gun into York's back.

'You are under arrest,' he muttered in York's ear.

'I never thought you'd have the guts to take me on,' York said, an odd tone in his voice that might have indicated admiration.

Ernest jabbed the gun in deeper, making York move forward. Then York got the hint and nodded to Dexter, who lowered his gun.

'I don't want to make this hard for

you,' Ernest said. 'So the two of us are going to walk out of here looking like two old friends chatting about the good times we've enjoyed.'

York laughed. 'I'm pleased you're making this easy for *me*, in the middle of my stockyard where I'm surrounded by my friends.'

Ernest shoved him on. 'Whether or not this is your stockyard has yet to be proved.'

★ ★ ★

'Open wide and eat the broth,' Cavanaugh said, holding out a brimming spoon.

'Not doing that,' Jarrett muttered through clenched teeth.

Cavanaugh smiled benignly. 'Don't be childish. If I want to, I can force you to take your medicine.'

'You can. I'm too weak to stop you.'

'I thought you'd be more subtle than that.' Cavanaugh made a show of taking a long step back, then cautiously he slipped the bowl on to the bed beside Jarrett's shoulder. 'But this is just broth. You can eat it yourself while you consider your choice.'

Jarrett eyed the bowl, but he didn't pick it up. As Cavanaugh had deduced, when he'd tried to move earlier, he'd found that the effect of the first bromide had worn off.

He had been trying to appear weaker than he was so that Cavanaugh would come close. Then Jarrett had reckoned he would need only one hand to throttle him.

His attempted subterfuge having been foiled, Jarrett moved up to rest on an elbow and poke the spoon around the bowl while he wondered how to detect whether the broth had been tainted.

'What choice?'

Cavanaugh moved over to a table and picked up two bottles. He waggled one at Jarrett, making the colourless liquid inside bubble.

'You've enjoyed a bromide and that helped you rest. If you take the bromide again, you won't be able to move and you'll be at my mercy until you do my bidding.'

'Nothing could make me kill for you again.'

Cavanaugh waggled the second bottle.

'In that case, I could give you the opposite, a concoction that will make your blood race. Your skin will feel like it's on fire, your muscles will twitch and your injuries will feel as fresh as if they'd only just happened. This torment will last for hours.'

Jarrett sneered; then, playing for time, he spooned the broth into his mouth.

'Or until I agree to do your bidding?' he asked with his mouth full.

'Or that.'

Jarrett swallowed another two mouthfuls, then gestured at Cavanaugh with the spoon.

'In that case I choose to have my blood racing. Maybe it'll let me move faster.'

Cavanaugh furrowed his brow, but Jarrett emphasized his point that he wasn't concerned by the threats by spooning the broth up to his mouth with rapid movements. So Cavanaugh moved over to the bed and held out the bottle in his left hand.

Steadily he poured a dribble of the liquid into the pool of remaining broth. Jarrett peered into the bowl as the colourless liquid dissipated quickly, while nodding approvingly as if Cavanaugh had just spiced his meal. He swirled his spoon around the bowl to mix the liquid in and then took a mouthful.

The broth didn't taste any different from before, but Jarrett licked his lips while tapping the spoon against the side of the bowl. Then he tried a different position on the bed, with the bowl resting on his chest.

He held the bowl with his right hand and gingerly edged his left hand to the spoon. He could raise the spoon for only a fraction and he had to lower his head to slurp the broth, but his success in using his left hand for the first time made him look triumphantly at Cavanaugh.

'This medicine sure does make the

blood race. I'm feeling better already and I'm much obliged.'

Cavanaugh gave him a narrowed-eyed look, then backed away.

'I'll return later. I don't reckon you'll be quite so arrogant then.'

Jarrett shrugged and ignored Cavanaugh as he concentrated on raising the spoon again. He kept his head lowered as he slipped the spoon in his mouth, then repeated the motion.

The door closed and he risked glancing up. Cavanaugh had left him, after all.

He leaned to the side and spat out as much of the broth as he could. He even wiped a finger around the inside of his mouth to clear the taste away, then he lay on his back, trying to work out what effect he thought it'd had.

He didn't judge that the concoction had done anything yet, but he figured that a small dose of something that made his blood race might give him a burst of energy first. Cavanaugh had taken his gun and anything else he might use as a weapon, but the chair was still in the surgery.

He tucked the spoon in his pocket so that he had something he could wield as a weapon while he planned how he would make the five-foot journey. He decided to find out first if he could walk.

By the time he'd used his good hand to complete the torturous process of dragging his legs off the bed and setting them down on the floor, he'd dismissed that possibility.

His legs just didn't have any strength in them and every movement made him feel as if a hot poker was being jabbed into his thighs. He feared the pain might be the first sign of Cavanaugh's concoction affecting him, so he settled for lowering himself to the floor.

Then, as he had done when moving along beside the railtracks on the night he'd been shot, he clawed his way across the floor. To his delight he reached the chair with only three squirming movements and he managed to climb into the chair without mishap.

Without the time to sit around and congratulate himself he put a hand to a wheel and pushed forward. Then, when the chair was moving, he swung his hand over and pushed the other wheel.

This manoeuvre dragged only a low squeak out of the chair and he reached the side of the door relatively quietly. He remembered the short journey from the next room to the back exit, and he thought he could accomplish it within a minute.

He didn't expect to reach the exit without Cavanaugh hearing him. So he didn't delay, but swung open the door.

Then he moved round to face the door, but Cavanaugh was standing on the other side. He looked down at Jarrett with a benign smile on his face.

'You didn't reckon you'd escape that easily, did you?' he asked.

Jarrett snarled and shoved the wheel, rolling himself at Cavanaugh, who stepped aside with ease so that the chair trundled by him. This direction would take Jarrett to the front of the building, but he'd seen steps down on to the main drag when he'd passed the building on his first day here.

He stopped the chair and embarked on the complicated set of jerking movements that turned him around. Cavanaugh watched him with amusement.

By the time Jarrett had finished his arm was aching and he slouched back in the chair, glaring at the doctor. The corridor that led to the back door was ten feet away, but Cavanaugh could block his route there by taking two steps to the side.

'I sure will make you pay for this,' Jarrett muttered, dismissing any idea of making the attempt to pass Cavanaugh.

'If you just do what I want you to do, there'll be no need for you to suffer any discomfort.'

'Why should I do that when you want me to shoot up innocent men?'

'The men aren't innocent, any more than the men you hunted for bounty. Just think of the bounty this time as being the cost of your treatment.'

Jarrett snarled. 'You're not treating me. You're torturing me.'

'I treated your wounds, and as for torturing you . . . ' Cavanaugh placed his hands wide apart. 'I'll do that if you don't give in, but I haven't done anything to you yet. I put only water in your broth. It was a test to see what you'd do, and I'm sorry to say you failed.'

'I don't believe you. I'm in more pain than before, just like you said I would be.'

'That's because you're out of bed and moving around.' Cavanaugh waggled a reproachful finger at him. 'Now go back into the surgery and rest and think. Later, we'll talk again about all the ways Quentin Stone wronged Lambert and why he deserves to die.'

Jarrett knew he'd never get a better chance to end this situation, even if his chances of escape now were slim, but perhaps, in response to Cavanaugh's revelation, he felt tired and he doubted he could even reach the bed.

He gave a brief nod. Cavanaugh smiled and moved towards him. He'd reached him when someone knocked on the front door.

Cavanaugh looked towards the front of the house with irritation as he took the back of Jarrett's chair. The knocking came again; this time it was insistent and growing louder with every knock.

'Sounds like trouble,' Jarrett said.

Cavanaugh muttered to himself as he moved round to the front of the chair.

'I'll see what the emergency is,' he said, turning away. 'While I'm gone, don't be foolish.'

Jarrett smiled faintly and let his head loll to one side. He had no doubt that this apparent sign of weakness wouldn't fool Cavanaugh, but the moment the doctor left he snapped upright and turned the chair towards the corridor.

He heard Cavanaugh shouting ahead to the person at the door that he was coming, but the knocking continued. Cavanaugh reached the front door as Jarrett moved off for the corridor. Over the sound of the squeaking wheels he heard the newcomer's demand.

'I'm looking for Jarrett Wade,' the man said. 'I reckon you patched him up.'

Jarrett groaned. He recognized the man's voice as being that of the man who had tried to kill him out at the shack.

12

'I have no idea who this Jarrett Wade is,' Cavanaugh said.

The doctor's reply had no effect; scuffling sounded as he was barged aside. Then determined and heavy footfalls sounded.

The newcomer would reach the back of the house within moments, so Jarrett put a hand to his chair's right wheel and shoved. He had been moving towards the corridor, but his aim wasn't perfect and he rolled towards the left-hand wall.

He shifted his weight to the right in the hope that this would cause him to veer aside, but the wheels had decided he would roll *that* way. He thudded into the wall, making him slip down in the chair, but the collision at least redirected him to run along beside the wall.

There wasn't enough space between the chair and the wall for him to slip his hand down and spin the left wheel, so he could only turn the right-hand wheel. Sitting hunched over and with a series of jerking movements, he scraped along beside the wall.

The effort taken in moving took his mind off worrying about his imminent discovery, and he flinched when the chair stopped making a pained screeching sound. He looked up to find he'd reached the end of the corridor: the back door was a few feet ahead.

Even better, he was heading directly for the door.

More obligingly than he could have hoped for the door flew open to its full extent, and he was able to roll out on to the open ground beyond. He was through before the door swung to again, missing the back of the chair as he rolled onwards.

Jarrett laughed at his success as the door slammed closed behind him, but his delight was short-lived when the chair ground to a halt in the soft ground. He shoved the wheel, but it didn't turn and when he looked around, the softer ground continued on either side for several yards.

Jarrett strained but, after failing to move, he accepted with a groan that he wouldn't be going anywhere. Back in the house clattering sounded in the surgery and the newcomer shouted something, getting a subdued response from Cavanaugh.

Jarrett hoped that it meant that the newcomer hadn't expected Cavanaugh's patient still to be here, but he would surely have heard his hurried departure. Either way, Jarrett had a few moments before he would be discovered, so he abandoned thoughts of getting away and looked around for somewhere to hide.

Two yards to his right was an old fence, which had fallen over to lean propped up against the wall. It was mouldering and had gaps, but it was the only object near by.

He tried to swing the chair towards the fence, but his efforts only caused the wheels to sink deeper into the dirt. He tried rocking the chair to free it but, as he could use only one arm, he wasn't strong enough to shift his weight by much and he succeeded only in slumping yet further down in the chair.

Then the chair toppled over sideways.

He crunched down on his side and spilled out of the chair. He tensed, waiting for the pain, but the softness of the ground meant that he landed relatively gently, and he was close to the fence.

With a lunge he grabbed the nearest fence post, then drew himself on. He had moved for only a foot when, looking round, he saw that his legs were entangled in the chair.

He strained harder, and his second tug dragged him clear of the chair. Then one more movement drew him beneath the fence.

Although he could no longer hear noises in the surgery, he felt vulnerable. He swung round and pushed his legs under cover. Then he reached out for the chair.

Three tugs drew the chair forward to cover the gap at the side of the fence.

Then he could do nothing other than lie behind it and hope he wouldn't be seen. A few moments later the door crashed open.

An irritated grunt sounded. Then rapid footfalls pattered away as the newcomer hurried along the back of the building in the opposite direction from where Jarrett was lying.

Jarrett reckoned that it meant Cavanaugh had been guarded in the details he'd vouchsafed and that the man hadn't expected him to be in such an immobile condition, but it also suggested that Cavanaugh would come outside within moments.

Sure enough, footsteps sounded in the doorway. The person stopped, then a grunt of triumph sounded as he turned towards the chair.

Jarrett frantically looked around for a weapon he could use. He saw nothing so, feeling foolish, he withdrew the spoon and brandished it before his face.

Then the chair was dragged aside.

He raised his head to glare out from

under the fence only to find, to his surprise, that Saul Cox was looking down at him. When Saul registered who was there, he raised his eyebrows in bemusement.

'Jarrett!' he exclaimed. 'What are you doing here?'

'Resting up,' Jarrett said, slipping the spoon away.

'And you?'

'The marshal arrested York Stevenson and York reckons his hired guns will go looking for someone who'd been injured when Lambert was killed.' Saul blew out his cheeks. 'I never expected that man would be you.'

'And Cavanaugh?'

'He's been knocked unconscious, but I reckon he'll be fine.'

A distant gunshot sounded. Jarrett couldn't help but think it was connected to the search for him, adding urgency to his next demand.

'In that case, help me up into this chair and we'll both head back to the law office.'

Saul righted the chair and took hold of Jarrett's left arm. This made him grunt in pain, so Saul held the chair firm while Jarrett dragged himself into it.

'You're sure in a bad way,' Saul said when Jarrett was sitting up.

'I'm in a lot better condition than some.' Jarrett gestured ahead with his good hand. 'Now head around the back of the Wild Horse saloon. If we're lucky we should be able to reach the main drag without being seen.'

Saul did as ordered, impressing Jarrett, as he had done the first time they met, with his ability to think quickly and clearly. He wheeled the chair past the back of the law office and came to the front of the building on the side nearest the door.

He glanced around the corner and waited for a few moments. Then he dragged the chair backwards on to the boardwalk and to the law office door.

He back-kicked the door open and drew Jarrett in, only stopping when they were five paces inside the room. Then he murmured in surprise.

Jarrett waved at him to close the door, but then he saw what had shocked Saul. Ernest Montague was lying beside his desk on his side; the blood on the floor and the open door to the jailhouse told their own story.

'Two of the hired guns must have broken York out,' Saul said softly, shock making his voice high-pitched, 'while the other gunman went to see Cavanaugh.'

'Three hired guns,' Jarrett said to himself as he resolved one mystery. He patted Saul's arm. 'See how the marshal is.'

Saul shook off his shock and hurried to Ernest's side. He put a hand to the marshal's shoulder and turned him over on to his back; the groan Ernest emitted made Saul sigh with relief.

'Leave me here,' Ernest murmured, fingering his bloodied stomach. 'Just get away.'

'I need to get you to help,' Saul replied. He waited, but when Ernest didn't respond he gestured at the jail-house. 'It looks like York's gone and that means his guns have probably left town too.'

This news appeared to reassure Ernest; he looked past Saul at Jarrett. He narrowed his eyes in confusion, then nodded in recognition. He waved Saul away.

'Fetch Doc Cavanaugh.'

Saul shot a worried look at Jarrett, who shrugged.

'You're a resourceful young man,' he said. 'Rousing Cavanaugh should be no trouble for you, and either way, it's time that sawbones did some healing.'

Saul flashed a last worried glance at Ernest, then hurried to the door, leaving the two men to consider each other.

'It's been a while, Jarrett,' Ernest said. He shuffled round to sit propped up against his desk, holding his stomach.

'It's been a while, Ernest,' Jarrett said. 'You're looking well, apart from the bullet wound.'

'You're looking old, even without the bullet wounds.' Ernest forced a tense smile. 'I assume you had a run-in with Dexter Pyle and his fellow hired guns.'

Jarrett looked aloft, nodding. 'So that's what this was about? I didn't know who shot me, but it was clear the gunman had a problem with me.'

The two men sat quietly as Jarrett pieced together in his mind the rest of the situation. He judged that Saul ought to have reached the surgery, when Ernest spoke up.

'Saul seems to trust and admire you.'

'I've been getting the same feeling about him.'

Ernest sighed. 'Then while Cavanaugh's fixing me up, tell him to keep out of sight for a while.'

This reminder of his recent experiences with the doctor encouraged Jarrett to wheel the chair across the law office. He found a gun lying on one of the desks, then wheeled himself back across the office. He stopped beside Ernest.

'The kid's resourceful. You don't need to worry about him.'

Ernest looked up, his narrow-eyed

gaze registering more than just the pain.

'York Stevenson is eliminating anyone who has a chance of inheriting Tyrone Hendrick's stockyard. I was unsure if that would include me, but after he was prepared to kill Gerald Gough, anyone with a link is in danger.'

Ernest winced and slid down the side of the desk, to lie propped up on an elbow. The speech appeared to have exhausted him, so Jarrett didn't burden him with an explanation of what had really happened to Gerald.

'So you fear that any kid of yours might be in danger, too?'

'Saul doesn't know,' Ernest murmured. He waved a vague hand at Jarrett. 'I told him I don't know.'

Jarrett assumed that Ernest had been referring to the matter that Saul had come here to resolve rather than to the stockyard, but Ernest then slipped down further, to lie curled up.

'Don't worry,' Jarrett said. 'While you rest up I'll look after the kid, and I'll look after the law office.'

Ernest murmured his thanks and Jarrett left him in peace. Presently, Saul returned with a groggy and apprehensive-looking Cavanaugh in tow.

Cavanaugh looked questioningly at Jarrett; in response Jarrett patted the six-shooter on his lap, then pointed at Ernest. Jarrett was pleased that despite their history, Cavanaugh's attitude seemed matter-of-fact as he knelt beside Ernest.

He offered Ernest reassuring words of the kind he'd first offered Jarrett; then he urged Saul to help him get the marshal back to the surgery.

'Will he be all right?' Saul asked.

'Of course.' Cavanaugh winked. 'I have my professional reputation to think about.'

He glanced at Jarrett, who gestured at the door with his gun.

'See to him and do a good job. Then come back here. I'm looking after the law office in Ernest's absence, so I'll need something for the pain.'

'I can look after the office,' Saul said.

'You have to sit with Ernest,' Jarrett told him. When Saul frowned, Jarrett pointed outside. 'And you have to guard him in case whoever shot him comes back to finish the job.'

Saul had been shaking his head, but this last order made him grunt with approval. Then, with him taking one arm and Cavanaugh taking the other, they dragged Ernest to his feet.

The marshal was able to walk, albeit crouched over and with a stumbling gait, and they moved on to the door readily. As soon as Jarrett was alone he rolled the wheeled chair behind Ernest's desk.

When he'd wheeled the chair up close he propped himself up with one elbow resting on the desk. He placed the gun on the desk, aimed at the door ready to take on York and his guns if they returned.

Then he settled down to wait for Cavanaugh to come back.

With nothing else to occupy his mind, he reckoned this was the right time to complete his understanding of the situation. He withdrew the metal case from his pocket and spread out the document on the desk.

With the other information he'd gathered since he'd last looked at the contract, this time he was able to decipher the legal terms with less trouble, and it seemed that Ernest had good cause to be concerned about Saul's welfare.

Tyrone Hendrick had written this document five years ago. He had given Lambert Stevenson five years to decide if he wanted the stockyard; if not Tyrone would sell it off and spread the proceeds.

The money would go to distant kin, various businesses associates, friends, and several people from Hamilton. These people included Ernest Montague, Gerald Gough, York Stevenson and, amusingly to Jarrett, Doctor Cavanaugh.

Twenty people were named and they'd each get an equal share. This meant Saul would inherit a twentieth part of the stockyard, if Ernest didn't recover and if he told the truth before the end.

With that matter resolved, Jarrett read the document again. This time he spotted a clause that he'd missed before. This simple statement made him smile, and he was still smiling when Cavanaugh returned.

'Ernest is resting,' Cavanaugh said, his eyes downcast. 'I hope he'll recover.'

'He'd better, or I'll be suspicious of what happened to him.'

'Ernest is my friend. Whatever you think about my actions, never think that I would cause him harm.'

'I accept that; curiously, even if you directed your ire at the wrong people, your actions appear to have spurred him on to become the lawman you wanted him to be.'

Cavanaugh nodded and moved over to sit on the edge of Ernest's desk.

'I brought something to help the pain.' He withdrew a bottle from his pocket and placed it on the desk. 'I hope you'll trust me enough to take it.'

'I will, because I'm not letting you out of my sight until I feel the benefit. If I don't, my last act will be to put so many bullets in you, even you wouldn't be able to save yourself.'

Cavanaugh pushed the bottle closer to Jarrett and stood back.

'And then?'

Cavanaugh looked at him hopefully, making Jarrett smile.

'And then,' said Jarrett, 'I'll need your help again.'

13

In the dead of night, the sounds of nearby cattle bustling in their pens was the only noise Jarrett could hear as Cavanaugh drove the open wagon into the stockyard.

Jarrett lay in the back, beside the wheeled chair. He'd found several sacks to lie on, but they hadn't been thick enough to stop him feeling every jolt on the journey. When Cavanaugh drew up outside York's cabin his good spirits had faded away.

'We're here,' Cavanaugh said, looking over his shoulder.

Jarrett used the side of the wagon to draw himself up and confirm that nobody was about. By the time Cavanaugh came round to the back and lowered the chair to the ground, his legs had stopped throbbing enough to let him attempt the manoeuvre of getting off the wagon and into the chair.

Then Cavanaugh wheeled him to the cabin, but he stopped at the door to look around again nervously.

'Quit panicking,' Jarrett said.

'We've been lucky to get this far without being seen.'

'Wagons and people moving around at night won't be suspicious here.'

'Anyway, I hope you've had enough help from me now.'

'I have, although I hope you've got more of that medicine to keep me going through the rest of the night.'

Cavanaugh nodded and handed over another bottle which, in the dark, looked no different from the other bottle. When Jarrett nodded approvingly, the doctor turned away.

'I wish you luck.'

'Don't worry about me,' Jarrett called after him. 'I intend to live through this, and tomorrow I'll check in on Ernest and Saul.'

Cavanaugh stopped for a moment; he didn't reply, but moved on to the wagon. Jarrett watched him until he'd clambered aboard and moved it on. Then he put his mind to opening the door of the cabin.

He fingered the handle, but that made the door inch open. Cautiously, he pushed the door fully open, but he could see nothing inside other than the desk set before the door and so he rolled back and forth until he'd lined himself up with the doorway.

He moved on through the doorway, then backed into the door to close it. That darkened the room, the only light being the small glow slipping in through the window.

He glanced around as he planned where in the room he would spend the night, then a rustling sound behind him alerted him a moment before a familiar voice spoke up.

'I'd hoped I'd get to see you again,' the man said. 'It's a pity not much of you is left.'

Jarrett tensed and cast his mind back to when he'd last heard this voice. He had spent so little time thinking about events prior to getting shot that it took him a few moments.

'Brett Cox,' he said. 'I can't say I hoped to ever meet you again.'

'You've got one chance to walk out of here alive,' Brett muttered. 'What did you do with my boy?'

Jarrett manoeuvred the chair around to face the corner where Brett was standing in the shadows. A stray beam of light illuminated gunmetal in his hand.

'Don't worry. Your investment is safe.'

Brett grunted. 'You appear to know plenty for a man who helped my son run away from home.'

Jarrett gestured down at his body. 'I know plenty for a man who went up against York Stevenson.'

Brett said nothing for a while. When he spoke again he lowered his six-shooter.

'I came here to get my son back before Ernest Montague could get his claws into him, but I heard that Lambert Stevenson had been killed. So I figured I'd have to get answers from York.' Brett gestured with his gun, inviting Jarrett to share the information he'd learnt.

'York shot up Lambert to stop him getting his hands on the stockyard. I got in the way. I intend for York to get in my way next.'

Brett nodded. 'And then, I assume, Ernest Montague will get the yard.'

Jarrett shrugged. 'I don't know. I reckon you probably know more about that than I do.'

'Before she died, Malvina told me everything she knew, but that was only what she'd learned from the time she knew Ernest. From that and from what I've learned since, I know someone will get the yard, and if it isn't York or Lambert, it could be Ernest.'

'And then one day Saul could inherit, and you'll benefit.'

'Don't judge me. For twelve years I looked after a kid that wasn't mine. I did right by him and he can do right by me.'

As Brett's voice rose in anger Jarrett thought quickly. Brett knew plenty about the situation, but as he was unaware of the document in Jarrett's pocket, Jarrett didn't know how he'd react to the news that he was fighting for Saul's share in the stockyard, not the yard itself.

'I'm sure you did, but there's no point in our fighting over that when the same man stands between us and what we want.'

Brett gazed at him, then gave a stern nod.

'I guess we can postpone sorting out our argument until later.'

Brett snorted a rueful laugh. He walked across the room to stand behind Jarrett. He rocked the chair back and forth experimentally, until he'd worked out how to use it.

Then he swung the chair around and stood it before the desk, facing the door, so ensuring that Jarrett would be the first thing anyone coming through the door would see. With a contented grunt to himself, he backed away to his former position in the corner.

'I assume you're letting me take care of York?' Jarrett said.

'Your role is to provide the next person through that door with target practice, but if you survive you can deal with York.'

'And your role is to hide in the corner and take the benefit from the hard work of others.'

'Be quiet. I'm only tolerating you so I can use you.'

Jarrett, having nothing else he wanted to say to this man, searched for a comfortable way to sit in the chair. When he'd settled down he found to his delight that his argument with Brett had taken his mind off his discomfort. He resolved to try to avoid taking Cavanaugh's medicine.

Instead, he looked straight ahead at the door.

He must have dozed as the next he knew light was streaming in through the window and he could hear sounds of activity outside.

He could now see Brett clearly. He

was sitting on the floor in the corner with his gun resting on a raised knee. Brett acknowledged him with a thin smile, then continued to listen.

In truth, after York had been broken out of jail and his hired gun had shot up the town marshal, Jarrett didn't know for sure that York would return here. But from what he'd learnt about the man, Jarrett judged that he would attempt to brazen out the situation by going about his business as if nothing had happened.

Sure enough, as the sounds of activity grew, several men approached the cabin. They were chatting to each other, so letting Jarrett identify one of the men as York. He could also hear Dexter Pyle, the leader of the men who had shot him.

He glanced at Brett, who was already on alert. Brett raised four fingers and in response Jarrett nodded and mouthed that one of the men was York.

Then he settled his six-shooter into his hand and aimed at the door. The men stopped outside the door and exchanged a few words before a small thud sounded and the door swung open.

They wouldn't have expected someone to have broken in, or for the door to be unlocked. So when the door opened it revealed the back of one of the gunmen, while another man was at his shoulder, looking ahead. York and Dexter were behind them.

York noticed Jarrett first. He moved to one side, causing the man nearest the doorway to swirl round. Jarrett had been aiming at the centre of the doorway, so he fired at this man, catching him in the side with a shot that made him knock into the door, sending it flying fully open.

As the man stumbled forward he blocked Jarrett's view of the second gunman, so Jarrett hammered a second shot into the wounded man, downing him. When the man fell he revealed the other gun-toter, who was sighting Jarrett with his own gun. Before he could fire Brett shot at

191

him, winging his left arm.

The gunman turned quickly and sighted Brett, who leapt forward, firing. Two gunshots rang out, but as both men were moving quickly they missed their targets.

By the time Jarrett had jerked his gun to the side and aimed at the gunman, Brett was tussling with him. The men stood close to each other each with his arms wrapped around the other; he didn't dare fire for fear of hitting Brett. He turned back to the door.

Through the doorway he couldn't see either York or Dexter, but his last sighting of them had been of York moving to the left and Dexter scurrying to the right. He assumed they were just beyond the door and picking their moment to burst in.

He trained his gun on the doorway and waited for either man to risk coming in, while to his right Brett and his opponent fought, each to turn his gun on the other. His opponent being wounded, Brett got the upper hand; the gunman appeared to accept that he was fighting a losing battle and he sought to break free.

The gunman kicked at Brett, then thrust his forearm into Brett's neck in a berserk action that made Brett lose his grip of his gun and stumble away. The gunman helped him on his way by shoving him backward making Brett's head thud into the wall.

Brett uttered a pained groan as he stood propped up against the wall for a moment. Then his eyes glazed and he slid down it.

With a grunt of anger the gunman jerked his gun arm towards him. Before he could fire Jarrett sliced a shot into the guntoter's back that made him fall forward to lie sprawled over Brett.

Jarrett trained his gun on the gunman, but neither he nor Brett moved; he figured that Brett had only been knocked out. When neither of the men outside had made a move, he punched in replacement bullets.

Then he aimed his gun at the

doorway and waited.

Outside, a murmured conversation ensued. Although Jarrett couldn't hear the words, he assumed that York and Dexter were sharing opinions and concluding that the situation had gone badly for their associates. Then York spoke up.

'Is that Jarrett Wade in there?' he asked.

'Sure is,' Jarrett said.

'You looked in a bad way.'

Jarrett didn't respond, leaving Dexter to speak up.

'In fact,' he said, 'he looks shot to hell.'

'The other two men who tried to kill me look in that condition,' Jarrett said. 'I reckon it's time you joined them.'

Silence reigned beyond the door and small changes in the light shining on the jamb made Jarrett reckon that Dexter and York were gesturing at each other as they planned their next move.

'I don't reckon so,' York said. 'Today is the day I finally end this situation and you're just a small obstacle in my path.'

'You'll never get your hands on this stockyard.'

'I will.' York laughed. 'But the only thing that should be on your mind is that you'll never get to leave my stock-yard alive.'

14

Jarrett waited for York and Dexter to risk coming in, but long moments passed without them making their move. He figured they would be able to call on help from the workers, so the longer they delayed acting, the worse his chances became.

'You won't ever get what you want,' Jarrett said, hoping to goad York into action. 'This yard isn't destined to end up in your hands.'

'I assume from that comment,' York said, 'that you saw the contract that Lambert never got to claim.'

'I have it on me. If you come in I'll let you read it.'

'I'm obliged for the offer, but I'll claim it later off your dead body.'

Jarrett snorted a confident laugh. 'If you knew what it said, you'd never want to claim it.'

'I know everything about that contract. After all, it was how this all started.'

Jarrett waited for York to offer more, but he didn't continue, confirming that he was hoping that when more workers arrived he could solicit help from someone who wouldn't ask too many questions.

'Amuse me, then. Tell me what you think is in the contract.'

'Tyrone Hendrick gave Lambert five years to decide if he wanted the yard. If he didn't, Tyrone would decide who else should inherit instead, and as I've spent those years doing good work, I deserve to own this place outright.'

'You may think you deserve it, but Tyrone must have a different opinion, as you won't get it.'

York laughed. 'Now I know you're lying. Five years ago Tyrone told me that if Lambert didn't take the yard, I was his second choice. He wouldn't change his mind.'

'Why are you so sure?'

'Because after he told me that, I

killed him.' York chuckled when Jarrett didn't retort. 'Nobody has ever questioned why Tyrone hasn't been seen since he left to enjoy his declining years, so I reckon I got away with that.'

'What did you do with him?'

'You won't live for long enough to see how I did it for yourself, but the thing about packing meat in a place like this is, it's easy to dispose of bodies and ensure nobody ever finds them.'

'Which means Tyrone wrote you out of inheriting this yard five years ago.' Jarrett chuckled. 'Clearly he was sure you wouldn't do a good job.'

'I'm not listening to no more of your lies.'

Jarrett judged that York's voice didn't sound as assured as it had done before, so he raised his voice.

'Now that Lambert's dead the yard is to be split between numerous people. You'll be pleased to hear you're one of them, but you'll get only a twentieth share of the proceeds, not the whole yard.'

'More lies! Tyrone never said nothing about that.'

York's arm came into view briefly as he gestured at Dexter, proving Jarrett's taunts were getting under his skin. He was getting angry enough to burst in. Jarrett aimed at a spot a foot in from the doorway, where he expected York to appear.

'That's because Tyrone hoped the yard wouldn't be divided up in that way. He gave Lambert the ultimatum that in five years he had to decide if he wanted the yard, or name the person who would inherit. If he couldn't decide, it'd be divided up.' Jarrett snorted. 'When you killed Lambert, you destroyed your own future. If you'd let me deliver the contract, Lambert would surely have named his own brother as — '

'No!' York muttered before he came storming in through the door.

Despite Jarrett's having a finger on the trigger, being prepared for York's move, York still moved so quickly he'd halved the distance to him before Jarrett got his wits about him.

He aimed at York and squeezed the trigger as York got him in his sights and fired. Jarrett was faster and more accurate, and his slug sliced up into York's stomach; at the same time Jarrett heard the back of the chair above his shoulder splinter as York's shot flew wide.

York ran on. Jarrett fired a second time, this time hitting his target high in the chest. York folded over, staggered on for another pace, then toppled forward.

He fell down over Jarrett's legs, making Jarrett cry out in pain. York's body rocked the chair backwards to knock against the desk, where it rested for a moment before it clattered down again on its wheels.

The movements jarred Jarrett's body and it took him a moment for his pain-narrowed eyes to focus. When they did he saw that Dexter had come into the cabin and he'd levelled his gun down at his chest.

Worse, York was lying as a dead weight over Jarrett's legs and lap, trapping his gun arm beneath him.

'How in tarnation did you manage to survive out at the shack?' Dexter muttered, glaring down at him.

Jarrett tried to point with his immobile left arm at his inside pocket where the contract rested, but he couldn't make his arm move. He used his hip to raise York's body slightly and that let him move his right arm forward a mite.

'You made a big mistake, that's how,' Jarrett said. 'Like your lousy brother did five years ago, just before I really shot him to hell.'

Dexter appraised Jarrett's trapped state and injured condition before he risked glancing aside at Brett, but Jarrett would get no help there. Brett was out cold, and when he'd fallen over he'd dropped his gun. It lay several feet away from him.

With a confident smirk on his face Dexter advanced on Jarrett, his careful actions seemingly designed to ensure there would be no mistakes this time.

'What big mistake?' he asked, settling his stance.

Jarrett smiled. 'Come closer and I'll explain.'

Jarrett leaned forward as if to speak to him, but he managed to move for only a few inches before he slumped back in the chair. That movement shifted York's position and let Jarrett move his right arm again.

Dexter looked him over, his suspicious gaze clearly weighing up what he reckoned Jarrett was planning to do before, with a shake of the head, he dismissed the matter. He aimed down at Jarrett's head.

'I guess I don't need to hear it. I'll settle for this time finally getting to shoot you to — '

Dexter didn't get to complete his taunt before Jarrett fired. The slug sliced up through York's jacket in the gap between his body and his arm, and hammered into the underside of Dexter's chin, cracking his head back.

For a moment Dexter stood up straight. Then his gun fell from his grasp and he toppled over backwards.

'You talk too much,' Jarrett said when he was sure that Dexter was lying still. 'That was your big mistake.'

After which statement Jarrett wasted no time in flexing his arm and squirming until York slipped off his lap to lie in a heap on the floor. Then he aimed his gun at the doorway, but even though sounds of consternation could be heard outside, he didn't hear anyone coming to investigate.

Despite this, he didn't reckon he should dally here for long. He wheeled himself over to Brett. He tried to reach down and shake him, but the activity of the last few minutes had exhausted him and he couldn't bend over.

He settled for wheeling the chair back and forth so that it nudged against Brett's side. It took him a dozen knocks before Brett stirred.

'What's happening?' Brett murmured, groggily.

'You've been resting up while I took on York Stevenson and his hired guns single-handedly.'

That comment provoked Brett enough for him to roll over on to his back and peer around the cabin.

'Who's left?' he asked, looking at York's body.

'Nobody that I know about, but I don't reckon we should wait around to find out who else might take exception to us.'

Brett levered himself up to his feet and stood stooped and feeling the back of his head.

'What do you want me to do?'

'Find a wagon and take me back to town.' Jarrett smiled. 'And then we'll see about securing your inheritance.'

15

When Brett pushed Jarrett into the surgery Ernest was sitting up in the same bed as Jarrett had occupied previously.

Saul was sitting on a chair at his side. He got up with a smile on his face that froze when he saw who had brought Jarrett back. For his part Brett didn't respond other than to wheel Jarrett on and set him down beside Ernest's bed.

Then he backed away without meeting Ernest's eye and faced Saul.

'What are you doing here?' Saul asked.

'I came to help you,' Brett said. 'And I ended up helping Jarrett defeat York Stevenson and the gun-slingers who shot up him and Lambert.'

Saul cast Jarrett an aggrieved look, presumably for having taken on this dangerous task after ensuring he was out of harm's way. Then he glared at Cavanaugh for not letting him know what was happening. Ernest, though, murmured in relief and settled down on his bed.

'So does that mean this is finally over?' Saul asked.

Jarrett nodded. 'It is.'

'And that means,' Brett said, 'it's time for us to go home, boy.'

'I'm not going anywhere with you,' Saul said, folding his arms. 'I intend to follow my own path and make my own life.'

Brett snarled at Ernest, making Ernest look away, although his pained expression suggested that, like Jarrett, he was in so much discomfort that he was struggling to concentrate on the situation.

'That man has nothing to offer you,' Brett snapped, pointing at Ernest. 'He abandoned your mother because he didn't have the guts to see anything through. Those aren't the lessons I taught you.'

Saul's eyes flared as he appeared ready to snap back a harsh retort, but then he lowered his head. When he looked up, his eyes were softer.

'You taught me some good lessons and I'm obliged for that,' he said in a conciliatory tone. 'You also taught me some harsh lessons and I'm obliged for that, too.'

Brett nodded. Cavanaugh shuffled across the surgery to stand before Ernest's bed, from where he could address everyone.

'From the sound of it, this matter has been resolved,' he declared with a smile. 'So now I've got two patients who are in need of care and rest, and they don't need to suffer this many visitors.'

'You heard him, Saul,' Brett said. 'We should leave.'

'I don't reckon he was talking to me,' Saul said.

Brett looked at Saul and Ernest in turn, his face reddening. Seeing that an outburst was inevitable, Jarrett raised a weak hand.

'Maybe I should tell everyone the full story, so they can make their decisions and leave me and Ernest to rest up.' He looked across to Brett, who mustered a nod, then he turned to Saul and Ernest. 'Brett got knocked out at the yard, so he didn't hear what I told York, but the stockyard is to be sold off and plenty of people will get a share in the proceeds.'

'Including me?' Ernest asked, his voice weak.

'Including you, and Doc Cavanaugh.' Jarrett paused while Cavanaugh shook a fist in triumph. 'And several people who are now dead would have benefited, so I guess it'll take a while to sort out the details.'

Everyone stood in silence, only Cavanaugh looking pleased and Ernest looking merely happy that he might be left in peace now. But Brett loomed over Saul.

'So now that you've heard the story, it's time you and I — '

'You didn't listen to me,' Saul shouted. 'I'm not going anywhere with you. I'm a man now, and besides, you're not my father.'

Brett snorted his breath through his

nostrils, his expression thunderous. Then he turned away smartly, but he used the motion to draw his gun and with a determined gesture he aimed it down at Ernest.

'That man's not keeping you here.'

'He's not. He's already told me that he knew my mother, but he's not . . . ' Saul sighed. 'He just knew her, that's all.'

'Except I know that was a lie, so now he'll tell the truth.'

Brett firmed his gun hand and with a pained murmur Ernest forced himself up on to an elbow to meet Brett's eye.

'Saul got the truth,' he said weakly. 'I'm not his father.'

'I read the letters.' Brett's gun hand shook as he struggled to suppress his rage. 'You're lying.'

Ernest closed his eyes, seemingly struggling to stay awake and leaving Saul to gesture angrily at Brett.

'The letters didn't say anything conclusive.'

'The ones *you* found didn't.' Brett

waited until that comment made Saul's mouth fall open in shock, then he chuckled. 'Ernest, and any kin of his, might not be in line to inherit the whole stockyard, but they'll still get a mighty tempting amount of money.'

'To you it may be tempting, but not to me. I don't want — '

'I don't care what you want! I wasted twelve years bringing you up and even if I have to wait another twelve years before someone puts a bullet in that so-called lawman, I will get what I deserve.'

Saul shrugged. 'It sounds to me that in that case I'll get the money, not you.'

'You'll do right by me, one way or the other.'

The two men glared at each other. Saul rocked forward on to his toes, looking as if he'd run at Brett, but Ernest spoke up, his voice more commanding than he'd managed since Jarrett had returned.

'If you two have finished with your argument, I'd like to say something,' he said firmly. 'I'm not this kid's father, which means if I should succumb either to this bullet wound or from everyone blabbering on until I die of exhaustion, he won't inherit nothing of mine.'

Ernest looked at each man in turn; then, with a determined sigh, he flopped back down on the bed. Cavanaugh nodded and moved forward with a hand raised to usher Brett away, but Brett barged him aside.

Brett moved round Ernest's bed to stand on the opposite side from everyone else and aimed down at Ernest's bandaged chest.

'You'll tell the truth or I'll put another bullet in you.'

Ernest closed his eyes and waved a weak hand at him.

'It seems to me that if I say what you want me to say, you might do that anyhow.'

'That's the chance you'll have to take, but I'm ending this here now.'

Ernest cranked open an eye to look at Saul, who looked at him hopefully. He bit his lip as he considered his reply, but just as he looked ready to respond,

Jarrett spoke up.

'I recently told Dexter Pyle that he'd made a big mistake,' he said, looking at Brett. 'It seems I'll have to tell you the same thing.'

'What big mistake?' Brett grunted, his gun hand tensing and his eyes narrowing with a look that said he was about to fire.

Jarrett raised the gun he'd drawn while Brett had been confronting Ernest and aimed it over the edge of the bed. Before Brett registered what he'd done, he fired low, catching Brett in the stomach and making him stagger backwards.

Then he fired a foot higher, making Brett drop his gun before he went sprawling over the bed. Brett clung hold of Ernest's leg for a moment until his grip loosened and he thudded to the floor.

'You talk too much,' Jarrett said.

★ ★ ★

'What are you planning to do about Doc Cavanaugh?' Jarrett asked later that night, when he and Ernest were the only people in the surgery.

'When I've recovered I'll get his full story,' Ernest said. 'But I reckon he just did what he'd been urging me to do for the last few years: to tackle the dark heart of this town. Gerald Gough was behind most of the trouble in Hamilton and my deputy broke most of the rules in ignoring that.'

'But he was your deputy.'

'I know, which means I'm as much to blame as anyone.' Ernest sighed. 'I don't have to explain nothing to you, but I accept now that I made mistakes. From now on I'll try to see things differently.'

'I'm pleased to hear it, and I'm even more pleased you're not excited about the thought of the money you'll now get.'

Ernest shuffled round on his bed to look at Jarrett.

'To be honest, even a week ago I'd have been delighted, but Saul told me about some letters I once wrote and they got me thinking about the man I used to be. The man who wrote those letters wouldn't have made the mistakes I've made.'

Jarrett nodded. Then they sat in silence for a while, letting Jarrett wonder whether Ernest would welcome his asking the question that nobody had asked after the encounter with Brett.

As he figured they'd both be here for a while and he didn't fancy skirting around the subject whenever Saul visited them, he shuffled to the edge of his bed, towards Ernest.

'So what's the truth about Saul?' he said, lowering his voice. 'Is he yours?'

Ernest shrugged, the action making him wince.

'That's a personal matter. The truth about that should remain between me and my kin.'

Jarrett considered this statement and decided that in a roundabout way it answered his question.

'Then why let Saul think he'll not inherit the money?'

Ernest smiled and contemplated the

ceiling for a while, looking as if he wouldn't answer, but then he shuffled closer and lowered his voice, too.

'Because I gave him the greatest gift of all, the one he wants. He's free to make his own way in the world and to do whatever he wants to do. He can go back to Brett's farm, stay here, move on, but whatever he decides, he won't be constrained by past problems that had nothing to do with him.'

'That's some gift.'

'It is, and of course I hope he comes back here from time to time. If things don't work out for him, I can always tell him the truth later.' Ernest flopped down on the bed and sighed. 'Perhaps by then I might be worthy enough for someone to call me a father.'

'I reckon you will be.' Jarrett smiled. 'And I reckon I might come back here from time to time.'

'Why?'

'Because this place has got me thinking about the man I used to be, too.' Jarrett lay down and felt the case in his pocket. It had been his constant companion for so long that now he felt no urge to remove it. 'It's made me realize there's still time to be that man again.'

We do hope that you have enjoyed reading this large print book.

Did you know that all of our titles are available for purchase?

We publish a wide range of high quality large print books including:
Romances, Mysteries, Classics
General Fiction
Non Fiction and Westerns

Special interest titles available in large print are:
The Little Oxford Dictionary
Music Book, Song Book
Hymn Book, Service Book

Also available from us courtesy of Oxford University Press:
Young Readers' Dictionary
(large print edition)
Young Readers' Thesaurus
(large print edition)

For further information or a free brochure, please contact us at:
Ulverscroft Large Print Books Ltd.,
The Green, Bradgate Road, Anstey,
Leicester, LE7 7FU, England.
Tel: (00 44) **0116 236 4325**
Fax: (00 44) **0116 234 0205**